EDDIE'S MENAGERIE

Books by Carolyn Haywood

CAROLYN HAYWOOD

EDDIE'S MENAGERIE

ILLUSTRATED BY INGRID FETZ

Troll Associates

Published by arrangement with William Morrow and Company,
Inc. For information address William Morrow and Company,
Inc., 105 Madison Avenue, New York, New York 10016.

First Troll Printing, 1987

Printed in the United States of America

10 9 8 7 6 5 4 3 2

ISBN 0-8167-1042-2

Contents

Dedicated with love
to my joy-inspiring friend,
Frances Whelan.

Chapter 1

EDDIE VISITS
THE PET SHOP

EDDIE WILSON loved animals, and animals loved Eddie. He had three dogs: an old English sheepdog named Hippie, a long-hair dachshund named Fritz, and a little black poodle named Patsy. Fritz was supposed to sleep in the doghouse, but he was so attached to

Hippie that he followed him everywhere. Where Hippie slept Fritz slept, and that was on the bottom of Eddie's bed. Patsy tried sleeping there too, but the other dogs took up so much room that she kept falling off the bed. There wasn't much room for Eddie either, but he managed not to fall off. Finally Patsy became satisfied to sleep in the doghouse.

Eddie also had a chameleon. His Uncle Ed, who lived in Texas, had brought it to Eddie. When his Uncle Ed gave it to him, he said, "A chameleon is a lizard, so you can call it either one."

"Well, I'm going to call him Bump, because his skin looks so bumpy," said Eddie.

Then Uncle Ed showed Eddie how Bump sometimes changed color when he was placed on different colored pieces of material. Eddie was delighted.

Not far from Eddie's school, at the corner of a narrow lane and the main street, there was a pet shop with an old red stable behind it. The pet shop was Eddie's favorite haunt. Hardly a day passed without his stopping in front of it. First Eddie pressed his nose against the window on the right side of the door and looked at the puppies. Then he went to the left side of the door and looked at the kittens. Eddie always saw a puppy or a kitten that he longed to buy, but he knew that his father and mother felt there were enough pets in the Wilsons' house.

One day, when Eddie was looking in the window of the pet shop, he decided to go inside. Of course, he wouldn't have dared to go home with anything alive, not so much as a ladybug.

As Eddie opened the door a bell rang. A moment later a man appeared. He was a little man with a very big head. His head seemed extra large to Eddie because it was not only bald but very shiny. Tufts of white hair stuck out over his ears, and a fringe of hair hung over the back of his collar. The man looked at

Eddie and grumbled, "Well, what do you want?"

Eddie thought he sounded very unfriendly. "I just came in to look around," he said.

"Oh, I know the likes of you," said the man. "I know you well."

This remark puzzled Eddie, but he said, "You have some nice puppies in the window, and some cute kittens too."

"Of course," said the man, "I never have anything but nice pets, and I don't need you to tell me."

"Mind if I look around?" said Eddie more timidly than before.

"You can look around," said the man, "but keep your hands in your pockets."

Eddie thought the request was a strange one, but he put his hands in his pockets and moved on. First Eddie looked at a large tank containing many varieties of goldfish. He thought they were beautiful. Then he looked at the birds in their cages and wondered whether his mother would let him have a bird. He would ask her.

Suddenly Eddie heard a sharp cry. I guess one of the puppies nipped another, he thought, and he walked over to look at some hamsters. In a cage next to them there was a beautiful black-and-white rabbit, which Eddie longed to pat, but he kept his hands in his pockets.

Next he looked at a little white mouse. Mice are cute, thought Eddie. He was surprised when he came upon a large jar that contained a live snake, and he wondered who would want a snake for a pet. Not me! thought Eddie. Eddie admired the collars and leashes that hung on racks. He looked at the toys for dogs and the toys for cats, but he was careful not to touch them.

The man stood in the center of the shop reading a newspaper. Finally he said to Eddie, "You in here to buy anything?"

Eddie turned to look at the shopkeeper. Now

he was wearing a most unusual hat. The crown was made of pie-shaped pieces that were red, white, and blue. Eddie liked the hat. He thought it was the most attractive one he had ever seen.

Again the man asked, "Are you in here to buy anything?"

"I'm sorry," said Eddie, "I just came in to look around. This is a swell shop."

"Humph!" said the man. "You kids waste my time, and some of you shoplift too."

"You want me to go?" Eddie asked.

"You can have a few more minutes," the man answered.

"Thanks," said Eddie, "I'm crazy about animals." Eddie moved to the back of the shop. There he was surprised to find shelves filled with toy animals. They came in all sizes. Some were tiny, no bigger than Eddie's hand, and some were almost life-size. Eddie's eye was taken by a toy spaniel that looked so real he

longed to pat it. There were bears and sheep, cats and a porcupine, owls and turtles, a lion, and even a little skunk. Eddie thought it was cute.

As Eddie turned away from the display, he said to the shopkeeper, "I like those toy animals. They're real neat."

"Umph," said the man. Then he added, "Look, kid, I can't stand here all day while you poke around. I have a dog to look after."

Eddie's ears pricked up. "A dog!" he exclaimed. "What's the matter with it?"

"Got hit by a car right in front of my shop. Looks like a broken leg," the man replied.

"Oh," cried Eddie, "that's terrible. It will have to go to the vet."

"No vet around here," said the man. "Nearest vet is forty miles away."

"What are you going to do?" Eddie asked.

"I'm trying to get hold of my wife. She'll come in and help me out."

Just then there was a cry that came from the back room, and Eddie recognized it as the cry of a dog in pain.

"What do you want your wife for?" Eddie asked.

"I want her to hold the dog while I put a splint on its leg," said the man.

"Can you do that?" Eddie asked in surprise.

"I can do it," said the man, "but I can't hold the dog still at the same time."

"I could hold the dog for you," said Eddie. "I love dogs."

"You're just a little kid," said the man. "My wife would know just how to hold it. It would probably jump out of your arms."

"No, it wouldn't," said Eddie. "Oh, please let me help you. Mr.—Mr.—"

"Cornball," said the man.

As another cry came from the dog, Eddie said, "Please, Mr. Cornball, I can hold it. I'm good with dogs."

Mr. Cornball looked at Eddie, and then he said, "Well, come along. We'll see."

Eddie followed Mr. Cornball into the back room, where the dog lay in a basket. Eddie knelt down beside it and murmured, "It's all right, fellow. It's all right. Mr. Cornball's going to fix you."

"It's a bitch," said Mr. Cornball.

"Oh," said Eddie, "what's her name? Do you know?"

"Missie," Mr. Cornball replied, as he lifted the dog out of the basket. "Sweet little girl she is. One of the nicest cockers I ever had in this shop. Sold her when she was a puppy to a little girl."

Eddie watched with interest to see what Mr. Cornball would do. He saw him bring in a small piece of wood from outside, and with a sharp knife he whittled the wood until it was smooth and just the right size to place against Missie's leg.

"Is that called a splint?" Eddie asked.

"That's right," Mr. Cornball answered, as he fitted the splint to Missie's leg. Then he asked Eddie to hand him the roll of gauze that was on the table. Eddie began to feel very important as he held Missie with his left hand and gave Mr. Cornball the roll with his right hand. Then he watched Mr. Cornball patiently and tenderly bandage Missie's leg. Eddie was impressed. "You're a real vet, Mr. Cornball," he said. "When I grow up, I want to be a vet and take care of animals too."

Mr. Cornball looked at Eddie. "I think you have the hands for it, young man," he said. "What's your name?"

"Eddie Wilson," Eddie replied.

"Well, someday you're going to be Dr. Edward Wilson," said Mr. Cornball, "Veterinarian."

Eddie was so pleased his ears turned bright red. "Can you fix horses too?" he asked.

"I shoe horses," Mr. Cornball replied. "I take care of them in the stable."

"Oh, I'd like to see you do that. I didn't know you were a blacksmith," said Eddie. "I know a poem about a blacksmith."

"I'm not a blacksmith," said Mr. Cornball. "The horseshoes come already made, and I fit them to the horse."

"I'd like to have a horse someday. That's what I want, a horse!" said Eddie.

"Fine creatures, horses," said Mr. Cornball. He had finished putting on the splint, and Missie no longer seemed to be in pain. "I must telephone Missie's owners and tell them where she is," said Mr. Cornball.

"I guess I better go now," said Eddie, giving Missie one last pat. "Thanks for letting me help."

As Eddie walked toward the door, he called back, "I like your hat, Mr. Cornball. I think it's swell."

"I'm glad you like it," Mr. Cornball said. "It keeps my head warm."

That night at dinner, Eddie said, "Boy, did I have a great time today!"

"Doing what?" his father asked.

"Helping Mr. Cornball at the pet shop to put a splint on a dog's broken leg, and do you know what?"

"What?" said his three brothers in a chorus, knowing that Eddie's news was sure to be surprising.

"Mr. Cornball said that I have the hands for being a vet," Eddie answered.

His brother Joe laughed. "I bet they call him Pop," he said.

"Why?" asked Eddie.

"Why, Popcorn Ball!" said Joe.

Eddie laughed with the boys, but then he turned serious again. "I think Mr. Cornball is right," he said. "I've just made up my mind. I'm going to be Dr. Edward Wilson when I grow up, and I'm going to be the best vet for miles around."

Chapter 2

BOY WANTED

About a week later, when Eddie went to look at the puppies and the kittens in the pet shop, he was surprised to see a sign in the window. It said, *Boy Wanted for Saturday Mornings.*

Eddie opened the door and walked into

the shop. Mr. Cornball was feeding the fish. He looked up and said, "Hello, Eddie. Nice to see you."

"Oh, Mr. Cornball, I see you want a boy. I'm a boy so could I have the job? I'd like to come every Saturday morning."

Mr. Cornball looked down at Eddie. "You couldn't take the job," he said. "You're not old enough."

"I'm ten," Eddie replied, "and don't you remember how I helped you with Missie? You said I had hands like a vet. Don't you remember? I could do a lot in the shop." Eddie was so excited he could hardly catch his breath.

"Do you want me to get arrested, Eddie?" Mr. Cornball asked.

"Why would you get arrested?" Eddie was puzzled.

"Didn't you ever hear of the Child Labor Law?" said Mr. Cornball.

"What's that?" asked Eddie.

"Why, it's a law that makes it illegal to hire any boy under sixteen years of age," said Mr. Cornball.

"But if you didn't pay me, couldn't I come?" Eddie asked coaxingly. "I just want to be with all these animals and help look after them. You don't have to pay me, Mr. Cornball."

"I couldn't do that, Eddie," said Mr. Cornball. "I couldn't have you working here for nothing."

"Yes, you could," said Eddie. "I'd watch out for shoplifters too."

Mr. Cornball shook his head and said, "Wouldn't be fair to take you on."

Eddie hung around the shop feeling very unhappy. At five o'clock, when it was time to close, Mr. Cornball said, "Time to close up now, Eddie. Get along."

Eddie looked up at Mr. Cornball and said, "Please, Mr. Cornball, please?"

"Can't do it," Mr. Cornball replied. "Can't hire a ten-year-old."

That evening at dinner Eddie told his family about his disappointment.

Rudy sat thinking for some time. Finally he said, "I'm sixteen. I could take the job, and you could come along."

"Great!" cried Eddie. "Dad's a volunteer fireman, and I'll be a volunteer detective. I'll watch the shop to see kids don't shoplift."

The following day was Saturday, so Rudy and Eddie went to the shop to see Mr. Cornball. Rudy explained that he was sixteen years old and he wanted to apply for the job at the pet shop.

Mr. Cornball asked Rudy a number of questions, and finally he said, "The job is yours, Rudy. Five dollars a morning. You can start right in today."

"That's very nice, Mr. Cornball," Rudy said, "but I'm sorry I can't stay this morning. I have a dentist's appointment."

"So," said Mr. Cornball, "I hire a boy and right away he has to go to the dentist."

"I'm sorry, Mr. Cornball," said Rudy, "but the appointment with the dentist was made a long time ago."

"Well, get along with you," said Mr. Cornball. "Off you go to the dentist."

"I'll stay, Mr. Cornball," said Eddie. "I'm going to come with Rudy and be the volunteer store detective. All the big stores have detectives. I'll be the volunteer watcher-outer. I'll keep my eyes open, and there won't be any shoplifting, not while I'm around. It's free, Mr. Cornball, all free."

"OK, Eddie," said Mr. Cornball. "Go ahead and watch. You might as well begin now. I have to do some accounts in the back room."

Eddie looked pleased. "I'll be here, Mr.

Cornball," he said. "Do you mind if I pick up the kittens? They look so cuddly."

"Pick 'em up if you want to," said Mr. Cornball. "Kittens don't break. Maybe you can sell one for me."

"Oh, great!" said Eddie. "How much are the kittens?"

"Three dollars," said Mr. Cornball. He patted Eddie on the head and went into the back of the shop.

Rudy left too, and in a short while a mother and her little boy came into the shop. The boy looked as though he wasn't more than three years old. His mother said to him, "You can let go of my hand, but don't touch anything."

Eddie watched the boy wander around the shop while his mother examined a lot of leashes that hung on a hook.

On a shelf low enough for the boy to reach were some cakes of soap for washing dogs. There were also packages of flea powder and tins of special dog food on display. Eddie saw the little boy pick up a piece of dog soap and start to pop it into his mouth.

"No, no!" Eddie cried out, as he ran to the child. Eddie took the soap from the boy's fingers and placed it back on the shelf.

The little boy yelled, "Candy! I want candy!"

"Well, this isn't candy. It's dog soap," said Eddie.

"Oh," cried the boy's mother, "how awful!" Then to Eddie she said, "Thank you. Chipper puts everything into his mouth."

Eddie took Chipper's hand and led him around the shop. He lifted him up so that he could see the kittens in one window and the puppies in the other. Chipper wanted to hold a white kitten, so Eddie lifted it out of the window and put it into his arms. The child was delighted. He purred like the kitten. "My kitty!" he kept saying. "My kitty!"

Eddie reached into the puppies' window to

straighten the food dish. As he did so, Chipper ran out the front door, which was open, with the kitten. Eddie dashed after him, calling out, "Chipper, come back! Come back!"

Just as he caught up to him Chipper dropped the kitten. That does it, thought Eddie. Now we'll lose the kitten. The kitten ran under a parked car, and Chipper was about to follow it when Eddie grabbed him by his belt. "No, you don't, Chipper," he said.

Chipper's mother was right behind Eddie. "No, no!" she kept calling. "Chipper, come here!"

With relief Eddie saw the kitten crawl out from under the car. Chipper pounced upon it and picked it up. "My kitty! Chipper's kitty!" he said.

"It is *not* your kitty," said his mother. "You must take it back."

Chipper began to cry as he was led back to the shop. "I want my kitty," he wailed.

Eddie finally got the kitten away from Chipper and put it back in the window while Chipper's mother continued her hunt for a leash that pleased her. When she found one, Eddie got Mr. Cornball and she paid him. Then Chipper, still crying, was dragged out of the door by his mother.

As the door closed on them, Eddie noticed that Chipper had a red cat collar in his hand. He went after them and said to Chipper's mother, "I'm sorry, but I think Chipper picked up a cat collar."

"Oh, dear, you naughty boy!" said his mother. She held out her hand and said, "Give it to me."

As Chipper gave the collar to his mother there were tears running down his face. "Kitty's collar!" he said. "Chipper wants kitty. Please, Mommy, please."

Chipper's mother stepped back into the shop. "Get the white kitten," she said to Eddie.

"Chipper seems to want it so badly I guess I'll have to buy it."

Eddie lifted the kitten out of the window and gave it to Chipper. While he held it, Eddie put the collar around the kitten's neck. At last Chipper was happy as he carried his kitten out of the store.

"Nice work, Eddie," said Mr. Cornball, patting Eddie on the shoulder. "Very nice."

Then Mr. Cornball went into the back room again, so Eddie was alone once more. Soon two girls came into the shop. Eddie thought they seemed about twelve years old, the same age as his twin brothers.

The girls looked at Eddie and said, "Hi!"

Eddie said, "Hi!"

As the girls walked to the back of the shop Eddie heard one of them say to the other, "The shells are in the back, Susie."

"Lead the way, Tina," Susie replied.

On a shelf near the toy animals there was

a tray filled with shells to be put into aquariums. The shells were of different colors, and they were very beautiful. There was also a large conch shell.

The girls rattled the shells and exclaimed to each other about them. "Here's a pretty one!" "Oh, look at this one!" "This is a beauty!"

Eddie decided to walk to the back of the shop to see what the girls were doing. When he reached them, the girl named Tina looked at him and said, "Who do you think you are?"

"I don't *think* who I am," said Eddie. "I *know* who I am."

Susie giggled.

"Well, who are you?" asked Tina.

"I'm Eddie Wilson," Eddie replied.

"Did you pick up these shells on a beach in Florida?" Tina asked.

"No," replied Eddie. "These shells belong to Mr. Cornball. He sells them."

"Oh," said Tina. " 'He sells seashells,' does he? Or is it 'he shells sea sells?' "

Susie laughed. "Oh, Tina, you're so funny," she said.

Eddie thought they were silly and walked away.

Soon Tina said to Susie, "Oh, Su, pick up the big shell and listen to the ocean."

In a moment Susie said, "Oh, boy, that's great. How much do you think this big shell would cost? I'd like to have it."

"Why don't you get it," said Tina.

"I haven't any money," Susie replied.

The girls fell very quiet, and Eddie decided to walk back and look at them.

"Here's Eddie again," said Tina. "He's a regular gumshoe. You can't hear him coming."

"Oh, Eddie's all right," said Susie. "Here, Eddie, listen to the ocean." Susie held the shell out to Eddie.

Eddie held the conch shell to his ear and watched Tina picking out beautiful little shells. He felt uneasy and wished Mr. Cornball would come back into the shop. After a few minutes Eddie left the girls and went to Mr. Cornball in the back room.

"Anything the matter, Eddie?" said Mr. Cornball.

"I'm not sure," Eddie replied. "A couple of girls are looking at the shells."

Mr. Cornball came back into the shop. He looked at the girls as he went by them and said to Eddie, "Do they want to buy anything?"

"Just looking," said Eddie.

"Just looking," Mr. Cornball repeated. "Well, I'm looking at them."

Soon Tina said, "Come on, Su, let's go," and the girls passed by Eddie and Mr. Cornball.

"Just a minute," said Mr. Cornball, and the girls stopped. "What's that bag?" he said to Susie.

"It's my book bag," said Susie.

"Let me look inside," said Mr. Cornball. "I'd like to see what books you're reading."

Susie looked scared as she handed her bag to Mr. Cornball. Before he opened it Eddie could see that there was a lump inside that was not a book. He was not surprised when Mr. Cornball pulled out the conch shell.

Susie hung her head in shame. "Now, young lady," said Mr. Cornball, "you are a shoplifter, and that is not a nice thing to be called, is it?"

"No, sir," said Susie, trembling. "Will I get arrested?"

"No, I won't call the police," said Mr. Cornball, "but if I ever see you in this shop again, I'll know that I have to keep an eye on you. You're just a common thief."

"I'm sorry," Susie said, close to tears. "I'll never do it again. I promise you."

"Very well," said Mr. Cornball. "If you want

to show you are really sorry, you can come and sweep my pavement every day for a week."

When the door closed behind the girls, Mr. Cornball said to Eddie, "I'm glad I have you as watcher-outer around here. That Susie almost put something over on us, didn't she?"

"I thought they needed watching," said Eddie.

The next Saturday, when Eddie arrived at the shop, he found Susie sweeping the pavement. "Hi, Susie," he said.

"Hi, Eddie," Susie replied. "Boy, did I get myself a job! I had to get up early every day this week to sweep this pavement before I went to school."

"Good exercise," said Eddie. "Puts roses in your cheeks."

"Don't kid me, Eddie," said Susie, swishing her broom.

Chapter 3

EDDIE FINDS A HAT

THERE WERE MANY REASONS why Eddie Wilson liked the place where he lived. In addition to the pet shop, he liked the park that was not far from his home. In the park was a small lake. Some people called it a pond, but Eddie liked to call it a lake. Whatever it was called, it was a good place for Eddie, his brothers, and his friends to race their model boats. In the winter it was a good place to skate.

Another attraction that brought Eddie to the park was a pony cart owned by an elderly man who was known as Gramp. The pony cart was very old, but the pony was young and lively. Every Saturday afternoon the pony cart was in the park to the delight of many children and especially to Eddie. It cost only twenty-five cents for a ride, so Gramp had many riders.

Eddie loved the pony whose name was Pumpkins, although usually he was called Punky. He always had something in his pocket, either sugar or an apple, for Punky. Before long the pony began to recognize Eddie, which delighted him.

Sometimes Eddie and his friend Jimmie went together for a pony-cart ride, and occasionally Gramp let the boys take turns at the reins driving Punky. Of course, as Eddie and the pony became friends, Eddie began to long more than ever for a horse. When he spoke about a horse to Jimmie, Jimmie said, "Why don't you want a pony?"

"Oh, I like ponies," said Eddie, "but a horse is better for riding and a pony couldn't pull a sleigh. I have to have a horse."

"Do you have a sleigh?" Jimmie asked.

"Yes, there was one in the barn when my father bought our place," said Eddie. "But what good is a sleigh without a horse?"

"I saw a sleigh once with flowers planted in it," said Jimmie. "It looked nice."

"Well, nobody is going to plant flowers in our sleigh," said Eddie. "Someday we'll have a horse, and then we'll take you for a sleigh ride."

"You're kidding," said Jimmie.

"You just wait and see," said Eddie. "Someday we'll have a horse. I just know we'll have a horse."

Beyond the park there were open fields. There the County Fair was held every year in the fall. Eddie looked forward to seeing the prize bulls, sheep, and hogs, although the hogs were a bit smelly. He also looked forward to the homemade cakes and pies that were on sale.

Eddie and his mother always went to the Fair the day it opened, because as Eddie said, "You get the best cakes the first day." This year was no exception, and their first stop was at the baked-goods table. Nearby was a booth displaying handicrafts, hooked rugs, quilts, and children's sweaters. While Mrs. Wilson waited for their baked goods to be placed in boxes, Eddie wandered over to the handicraft booth.

Suddenly he noticed a hat hanging on the side of the booth, and he began to inspect it. The hat was exactly like Mr. Cornball's, which Eddie had so admired. The crown was made of the same pie-shaped pieces in the same red, white, and blue colors. To Eddie's great sur-

prise, however, there were the white letters
E-D-D-I-E on the blue visor.

Eddie called to his mother, "Ma, come see!
Come see!"

Mrs. Wilson picked up her boxes and went
to see what was exciting Eddie. "Look, Ma,"
said Eddie. "This is my hat. I have to have this
hat. It's the greatest!"

Mrs. Wilson looked at the hat. She, too, was
surprised. "Now, Eddie," she said, "You can't
go around in a hat like that."

"Ma, I don't want a hat *like* that. I want *this*
hat. See? It has my name on it."

Mrs. Wilson saw quite plainly that Eddie's
name was on the hat, but she said, "Oh, Eddie,
it's much too loud."

"No, it isn't," said Eddie, "and I'm going to
have it. It's just like Mr. Cornball's."

Eddie leaned over the counter and pointed
the hat out to the woman in the booth. "How
much is this hat?" he asked.

"Oh, *that* hat?" the woman replied. "Do you like that hat?"

"I think it's super," said Eddie. "Mr. Cornball at the pet shop has one just like it."

The woman back of the counter laughed. "Oh, so you saw Mr. Cornball's?" she said. "Well, I'm Mrs. Cornball, and I made his hat. You see, Mr. Cornball doesn't have very much hair and his head gets cold. He used to wear a black cap, but he kept losing it all the time. He would put it down, and then he couldn't see it because it was black. So I decided to make him a hat that he could see."

Mrs. Cornball held the hat out to Eddie and said, "I made this one just like Mr. Cornball's. Both of them are sewed the way patchwork quilts used to be. They're very special hats. There's not another one like them. It was my grandson's idea to put the name Eddie on the visor. I hoped that someone named Eddie would come along and buy it."

"Well, how much is it?" Eddie asked. "My name's Eddie."

"Oh, how nice," Mrs. Cornball exclaimed. "So you're Eddie! I'm afraid it's a little expensive, but you see it's all made by hand."

"Well, how much is it?" Eddie was so excited he could hardly stand still.

"Five dollars," Mrs. Cornball replied. "You see, I have to get five dollars for it since it's all made by hand."

"Oh, Eddie!" said his mother. "You're not going to buy that hat, are you? How are you going to pay for it?"

"It's my hat, Ma," Eddie replied. "It has my name on it. I have five dollars saved from my allowance. I bet if *you* ever found a hat with your name on it you would buy it."

"I hope I never find a hat with my name on it!" his mother replied.

Eddie handed the five-dollar bill to Mrs. Cornball as he put the hat on.

"Thank you," said Mrs. Cornball. "It looks good on you. It surely is your hat."

"That's what I think," said Eddie, as he walked away with his mother.

Now that the hat belonged to Eddie he only removed it when he went to bed. At school on Monday it created some excitement. Eddie had to answer the question, "Where did you get that hat?" over and over again. It was not only the envy of the girls but of the boys as well. Eddie would have liked to have worn the hat all day in school, but as he couldn't he hid it in his desk.

The following Saturday afternoon, after he was finished at the pet shop, Eddie went with Jimmie to the park for a ride in the pony cart. Eddie had an apple for Punky in one of his pockets. In the other pocket he had Bump, his chameleon.

The boys took the bus to the park. When they

were seated, Eddie said, "I brought Bump along," and he took his chameleon out of his pocket and showed it to Jimmie.

"I want to see it change color," said Jimmie. "Put him on my plaid jacket."

Eddie put the chameleon on Jimmie's jacket.

Jimmie looked at it and cried out, "He didn't turn plaid."

"I guess that's because he isn't Scotch," said Eddie. "He's a Texas chameleon. He only turns one color at a time."

When Eddie and Jimmie reached the park, they ran to Gramp and the pony cart. "Hi, Gramp!" Eddie called out. "I brought an apple for Punky."

"He'll be pleased," said Gramp.

Eddie stepped up to the pony and spoke softly to him as he munched the apple.

When the boys got into the cart, Gramp said, "There's a strong wind today."

In a moment they were off for a ride. "Go

fast," said Eddie to Gramp. "I like to go fast."

"All right," Gramp replied. "Hold your hat."

As the pony cart reached the road that circled the lake Eddie could see many children busy with their boats around the edge. Eddie was not holding his hat. Suddenly the wind caught it and it blew off. "Hey, wait!" Eddie cried. "Wait! I've lost my hat."

Gramp said, "Whoa," and pulled the pony to a stop.

Eddie ran after his hat, but to his horror he saw it fall into the lake. Then he saw a boy lean out over the water to rescue it. Suddenly there was a terrific splash, and water flew into the air. The boy had fallen into the lake.

When Eddie reached the edge of the lake, the boy stood up in the water and Eddie recognized his classmate Larry. "Oh, Larry!" cried Eddie. "You're awful wet."

With water dripping from his clothes, Larry

said, "Yeah, it's very wet water. Sorry I missed your hat, but now that I'm in the lake I'll see if I can get it."

"Oh, thanks," said Eddie. "It's right behind you."

Larry looked behind him, and with more splashing he reached Eddie's hat.

When he handed it to Eddie, Eddie said, "Thanks a lot. I hope it isn't cold in the water."

With his teeth chattering, Larry said, "I-t-t-t-s O-O-O-K-K-K."

Just then Gramp and Jimmie drove up in the pony cart. "Are you boys in trouble?" said Gramp.

"Larry rescued my hat from the lake," said Eddie, "but he fell in and got awful wet."

Gramp looked at Larry. "Where do you live?" he asked.

"Just on the other side of the lake," said Larry. "It won't take me long to run home."

"Run, nothing," said Gramp. "You jump in the cart, and I'll have you home in a jiffy. You have to get out of those wet clothes."

As Eddie watched Larry, dripping water, step out of the lake he wished he had something to give him for rescuing his hat. But he couldn't think of anything. Suddenly he felt Bump stir in his pocket, and he pulled him out.

"Oh," cried Larry, "you have Bump with you. He's great!"

"Would you like to have him?" Eddie asked.

"Do you mean it?" said Larry. "Do you mean for keeps?"

"Yes, sure," said Eddie. "You'll take good care of him, won't you?" Eddie sounded a little wistful.

"Oh, yes," said Larry. "What do I feed him?"

"You have to catch flies for him," said Eddie.

"I can only catch flies in the summertime. In the winter I can only catch snowflakes," said Larry.

"They won't do," said Eddie. "You'll have to buy mealworms for him. He likes mealworms."

"I'm glad I don't have to catch the mealworms," said Larry.

"No, you buy them at Mr. Cornball's," said Eddie.

"Does Bump need a litter pan like the cats?" Larry asked.

"No, you keep him in an aquarium, but be sure it has a screen over the top. Otherwise, he'll climb out and up the wall."

"That would scare my mother so much *she'd* walk up the wall," said Larry.

Eddie handed Bump to Larry, and Larry said, "Thanks, Eddie. When Bump grows up, perhaps he'll turn into an alligator."

"Alligator!" exclaimed Eddie. "Bump's a chameleon."

"I think he looks a little like an alligator," said Larry.

Eddie gave Bump a final stroke and said, "Good-bye, Bump."

After Larry and Gramp had driven away, Jimmie said to Eddie, "How could you, Eddie? How could you give Bump away?"

"Well, you see Larry rescued my hat when it blew into the lake. I wanted to give him something."

"He only fell into the water," said Jimmie. "He didn't drown."

"He got awful wet," said Eddie.

"You gave him Bump just for getting your old hat?" said Jimmie.

"It isn't an old hat. It's a new hat," Eddie said. Eddie looked it over carefully and said, "I guess it will be all right when it gets dry. You see, I can get another chameleon from my Uncle Ed when he comes up from Texas, but I could never get another hat like this one. It's very special."

"You know what, Eddie?" said Jimmie.

"What," said Eddie.

"I've been thinking," said Jimmie. "Wouldn't Larry be surprised if Bump did grow up to be an alligator."

"Jimmie, you're nuts," said Eddie. "How could he be an alligator when he's a chameleon?"

Chapter 4

ROLAND'S SKUNK

EDDIE KEPT URGING his friend Roland to come with him to the pet shop, but Roland didn't seem anxious to go.

One day when Eddie spoke to Roland about the pet shop he said, "Nicest puppies you ever saw and the cutest kittens. It's a swell place.

Why don't you come some Saturday morning when I'm there?"

Roland finally appeared, and Eddie was glad to see him. "Hi, Roland!" Eddie called out. "Let me show you around."

"OK," said Roland.

Eddie pointed out the best puppies and the nicest kittens. He showed Roland the birds he liked the best and the beautiful fish.

When Roland saw the jar containing the snake, he exclaimed, "Snakes! Who wants snakes?"

"I guess they're OK," said Eddie. "After you get used to them."

"Not for me!" said Roland.

"Mr. Cornball has worms too," said Eddie. "He keeps them in boxes out in the stable."

"Pet worms!" exclaimed Roland.

"They're not for pets," said Eddie. "People buy them to put in their gardens. They crawl around in the dirt and break it up. It's called cultivating. Mr. Cornball calls all the worms George."

"Why?" Roland asked.

"Oh, because people always say 'Let George do it'! Mr. Cornball sells thousands of worms."

"You're kidding," said Roland.

"It's the truth," said Eddie.

Now Eddie led Roland to the counter where the toy animals were displayed. "I think these toy animals are great," said Eddie.

"This little skunk is cute," said Roland, picking it up. "I like skunks."

"I don't like the way they smell," said Eddie.

"This one doesn't smell," said Roland. "I wish I could have it."

"Why don't you buy it?" said Eddie. "It costs two dollars."

"Two dollars!" exclaimed Roland. "Where do you think I could get two dollars?"

"Couldn't you ask your father for it?" Eddie replied.

"Do you think my father is a millionaire?" said Roland.

"The skunk isn't two million dollars," said Eddie. "Just two dollars."

"Might as well be two million," said Roland, fondling the skunk. "The only way I could get this skunk is to steal it."

"You know what skunks do if you try to steal 'em?" said Eddie. "They go swoosh and make a smell."

"Quit spoofing me," said Roland. "This one doesn't make a smell."

"If you tried to steal it, it might," said Eddie.

"Go on!" said Roland. "I'm just kidding."

One morning when Eddie got to school he found Roland surrounded by some of the children in the class. Eddie joined the group and looked over Roland's shoulder. "What's up?" Eddie asked.

"Roland has a cute little toy skunk," said Gloria.

Eddie looked at the little skunk. It was exactly like the one Roland had admired among the toy animals in the shop. "Where did you get it, Roland?" Eddie asked.

"My sister gave it to me," Roland replied.

"I didn't know you had a sister," said Eddie.

"Sure I have," Roland answered. "She's grown up and married. Has a baby too. That makes me an uncle."

Just then the bell rang for school to begin. Mr. Jeffrey called the class to order, and the arithmetic lesson started. It was one of those mornings when Mr. Jeffrey wrote what he called "problems" on the blackboard. "Mary had seven apples," and they went on and on. Eddie couldn't keep his mind on the work.

When the arithmetic lesson was over, Eddie had missed every problem. They were all wrong. Mr. Jeffrey was surprised and said,

"Eddie, you didn't have your mind on those problems this morning."

"Sorry, Mr. Jeffrey," said Eddie.

"You were just woolgathering," said Mr. Jeffrey.

Eddie decided that Mr. Jeffrey was right, for his mind was on Roland's little skunk. Every time he thought of Roland he wondered whether Roland had stolen the toy. He couldn't stop worrying about his friend.

Several days later Mr. Jeffrey opened the morning by telling the class that Mr. Butler, the principal of the school, had received complaints from the shopkeepers in the town that children had been shoplifting in their stores. Mr. Jeffrey talked a long time about the situation and finally said that he hoped no one in his class was guilty of such behavior.

Eddie glanced across the room at Roland. Roland certainly looked innocent, but still Eddie was troubled.

At lunchtime Eddie said to Roland, "That shoplifting is pretty bad."

All Roland said was "yep" and he picked up his lunch tray and carried it away.

Roland brought the toy to school every day. Mr. Jeffrey told him several times that he must keep it inside his desk, but Roland wouldn't leave it alone. Eddie noticed that Roland was always sneaking a look at his little skunk.

One day Mr. Jeffrey took it away from Roland, and Roland frowned and looked very unhappy.

"I'll give it back to you at the end of the day," said Mr. Jeffrey. "This skunk takes up too much of your time and thought. You don't finish your work."

Eddie thought the little skunk was taking up too much of *his* time and thought too.

One day Roland said to Eddie, "I don't know what I'm going to do. My sister's birthday is next Saturday, and I want to buy her a box of candy. My sister is good to me, but a box of candy costs two dollars, and I don't have any money." Roland's brow was wrinkled. "Sure wish I could buy that box of candy."

Eddie thought for a moment. He had his weekly allowance of two dollars in his pocket. He made his decision quickly. "Tell you what, Roland," he said. "I like that little skunk you have. I'll give you two dollars for it."

Roland's face brightened. "You will?" he said. "Eddie, you're the greatest."

Eddie handed the two dollars to Roland, and Roland gave the little skunk to Eddie. He put it in his pocket.

After school, Eddie walked alone to the pet shop. He opened the door and went inside. The bell hadn't stopped ringing before Mr. Cornball appeared. "Oh, it's you," he said. "How are you, Eddie?"

"I'm fine," Eddie replied. "You taking care of any dogs today?"

"Not today," Mr. Cornball replied.

Eddie looked at the puppies, and he looked at the kittens. He moved slowly toward the back of the shop, looking at all of the pets on his way. As he got near the shelf where the toy animals were displayed he kept his hand firmly gripped on the little skunk in his pocket. Eddie wished Mr. Cornball would go back into the other room, but Mr. Cornball stayed in the shop, stopping first at one cage and then at another. He fed the fish and changed the water in all of the birds' cages.

Finally Mr. Cornball said, "I'll have to get the scissors and cut the parakeet's nails. They're much too long. I'll be back in a jiffy. If anyone comes in, you keep your eye on 'em."

"OK," Eddie answered, as Mr. Cornball disappeared into the back of the shop.

Quick as a flash Eddie pulled the little skunk out of his pocket and placed it on the shelf among the other animals. Eddie found that he was trembling, yet he accomplished what he had come in to do. Roland might be a thief, but the toy animal was back where it belonged.

As the days passed Roland kept asking Eddie about the skunk. "You never bring the little skunk to school," Roland would say. "Don't you like it?"

"Sure I like it," Eddie would reply, "but I wouldn't want Mr. Jeffrey to take it away from me."

"Where did you put it?" Roland asked.

"Oh, I found a good place for it," Eddie replied.

"You didn't put it where your dogs could get it and chew it up, did you?" Roland asked.

"Oh, no, I wouldn't let the dogs chew it up," Eddie answered.

One Saturday morning Eddie got to the shop ahead of Rudy. When Mr. Cornball saw Eddie, he said, "You good at arithmetic, Eddie?"

"Pretty good," Eddie replied.

"Well, I'm puzzled," said Mr. Cornball, taking off his hat and scratching his head.

"What about?" Eddie asked.

"You see, I had ten of these little skunks the first of the month. I know 'cause I made a note of it in my ledger. Well, I sold one of them to a young woman. I remember her. She had a baby in her arms. She said she was buying it for her little brother, because he was crazy about skunks." Mr. Cornball chuckled. "Must say, they're not my favorite animal, but if the kid likes them, that's good for business."

Eddie was getting more and more interested as Mr. Cornball went on. "Now," he said, "if I had ten and sold one, I should have nine left. Right?"

"Right," Eddie agreed. "That's what Mr. Jeffrey calls a problem."

"It's a problem for sure," said Mr. Cornball,

"because I've counted them over and over and there are always ten."

This information brought joy to Eddie. Now he knew that Roland was not a shoplifter. Roland had told the truth when he said his sister had given it to him.

Poor Roland, thought Eddie, he no longer has his skunk.

Then Eddie told the whole story to Mr. Cornball.

Mr. Cornball laughed. "Well, Eddie," he said, "I'm afraid you're taking your job as watcher-outer too seriously. Ever since Susie tried to steal that shell, you've become too suspicious."

"I guess you're right, Mr. Cornball," said Eddie. "That's not so good. I'll be more careful not to overdo my job."

"That extra skunk I have I'll give back to you," said Mr. Cornball.

"Thanks, Mr. Cornball. I'll give it to Roland for Christmas," said Eddie.

"He'll like that, and Christmas is on the way. It's already the first of November."

Chapter 5

PATRIOTIC GLORIA

Eddie woke up one morning and heard the rain beating on the roof over his head. His eyes sought out his treasured hat. It was where he had left it on the chair beside his bed. He began to wonder what he could do to protect his hat against the pouring rain. Should he leave it at home rather than wear it to school? He decided against this course of action. After all, the house might be robbed while he was in school, and any robber would be sure to steal his hat. He thought of carrying it in his schoolbag, but if he packed it up with his books, it would come out full of wrinkles. He didn't want a wrinkled hat, so he decided he would have to think of some other way to protect it. Perhaps his mother would have an idea.

As soon as he sat down at the breakfast table, he said, "Ma, what about my hat?"

"Well, what about it?" his mother asked.

"It'll get wet," Eddie said.

"I'll lend you my rain hood," said his mother.

"You will, Ma? That's great," said Eddie.

Eddie's brothers dashed off as soon as breakfast was over, but Eddie had to wait while his mother covered his hat with her rain hood. When she put it on him, she was careful to cover his hat completely. As she tied it under his chin, she said, "We don't want this to blow away in the high wind."

"Thanks, Ma," said Eddie. "Thanks for lending it to me. I'll be careful of it." He put on his yellow slicker and went to join Jimmie and his brothers at the bus stop.

When Jimmie saw Eddie, he said, "Why are you done up like that?"

"Don't want to get my hat wet," Eddie replied.

"Don't you have a hood to that coat?" Jimmie asked.

"I lost it," Eddie answered.

Eddie's brother Rudy looked at Eddie and said, "Did you look at yourself?"

"No," said Eddie. "Why?"

"You look sort of cute," said Rudy.

"What do you mean 'cute'?" asked Eddie, as the bus drove up.

Before Rudy could answer, the door opened

and Eddie stepped into the bus. Mr. Jolly, the bus driver, looked at Eddie and said, "Well, who do we have here?"

"Little Bo Peep," said Rudy.

"Ya," said Joe, "but he lost his sheep."

"Shut up!" said Eddie.

The children on the bus all began to giggle.

As Eddie made his way through the bus he pulled off his mother's rain hood. Most of the seats were filled, for no one was walking to school today. Finally Eddie found a seat beside Gloria.

"Hi, Eddie!" said Gloria. "You're going to get your nice hat wet."

"I know," Eddie replied. "Ma gave me her rain hood." Eddie held up the hood, which was now dripping water.

"Why did you take it off?" Gloria asked.

"Oh, my brothers made fun of me," said Eddie.

"Well, it's a shame to get that swell hat wet," said Gloria. "It's beautiful. Real patriotic."

Eddie was pleased. "You think so, Gloria?"

"Sure do," replied Gloria. "Wish I had one just like it."

"It's not a girl's hat," said Eddie.

"I don't care. I like it," said Gloria. "My mother buys me boys' sweaters. Why shouldn't I wear a boy's hat?"

The bus bounced along while Eddie and Gloria sat in silence. Just before they reached the school, Gloria said, "Tell you what, Eddie. It would be a shame to get that hat wet. Why don't you let me wear it with your mother's rain hood, and you can use my umbrella."

"OK," said Eddie. "That's nice of you, Gloria." It didn't occur to Eddie that he could keep his hat dry under Gloria's umbrella. He just handed his hat and his mother's hood to Gloria, who put them over her mop of red hair.

Soon the children stood up to get off the bus. Gloria handed her umbrella to Eddie. "This will keep your head dry," she said, "and I'll keep your hat dry."

"Thanks," said Eddie. "You'll give it back to me when we get into school, won't you?"

"Oh, sure," Gloria replied, "but if it's still raining when school's over, you better let me wear it home. You can take my umbrella."

"Maybe it won't be raining," said Eddie, as he followed Gloria to the door of the bus.

Gloria stepped out into the pouring rain. Eddie followed and immediately put up the umbrella. But he hadn't taken three steps when a great gust of wind caught the umbrella and blew it out of his hands. The wind carried it to the top of an iron fence in front of the school. There it hung on a spike. Eddie reached up to get it, but as he pulled it free he heard the umbrella rip. With horror Eddie saw there was a big tear in the cover.

Eddie was examining the umbrella when Rudy came along. "What's the matter, kid?" asked Rudy.

"Gosh," said Eddie, "look what happened to Gloria's umbrella."

"Just a piece of junk now," said Rudy, "but maybe you might call it 'valuable property.'" Eddie was a great collector of junk, which he always considered valuable property.

Eddie didn't think this remark of his brother's was funny. "I guess the umbrella was valuable property to Gloria," he said.

"Might as well get rid of it," said Rudy, pointing to a trash bin nearby.

"Get rid of it!" Eddie exclaimed. "This is valuable property."

Rudy looked at it and said, "What's valuable about it? It's just a piece of junk."

"You'll see," said Eddie.

"What *you'll* see," said his brother, "is that

you'll have to buy Gloria a new umbrella. She'll be hopping mad when she sees this wreck."

When Eddie reached the classroom, he said to Gloria, "I'm sorry about your umbrella, but it blew away and got caught on the fence."

"Oh, Eddie," Gloria cried, "that's too bad. I guess you'll have to get me a new umbrella."

"I thought you would say that," said Eddie. "I can't get it right away."

"That's OK," said Gloria. "I'll keep your hat, and when you give me an umbrella, I'll give you your hat."

Eddie didn't think much of this idea. "Oh, Gloria," he said, "you'll take good care of my hat, won't you?"

"Of course," replied Gloria. "I'm crazy about this hat. I wouldn't let anything happen to it. It's so patriotic."

Eddie looked at the valuable property in his hand and at his hat, and he wondered how long it would be before he got his hat back.

The following day Jimmie said to Eddie, "I see Gloria is wearing your hat. She never takes it off. How come you gave it to Gloria?"

"I didn't give it to her," Eddie replied.

"Well, she keeps talking about it as though it were hers. Calls it her 'patriotic hat.' She thinks she's the Goddess of Liberty."

"That's right," said a girl named Sylvia, who was standing nearby. "Gloria says she's going to wear it in the Fourth of July parade next year."

"She is, is she?" said Eddie. "Well, it's my hat and I'm going to wear it in the Fourth of July parade."

"I don't know how you're going to get it away from her," said Jimmie. "She's stuck on that hat."

"You just wait and see," said Eddie.

The following Saturday Eddie took Gloria's umbrella with him when he went to the pet shop. "Hello, Eddie," said Mr. Cornball. "Where's your hat?"

"Oh, Mr. Cornball," said Eddie. "Some girl has my hat, and she won't give it back to me until I get her a new umbrella."

"How come?" said Mr. Cornball.

Eddie told Mr. Cornball the whole story. When he finished, Mr. Cornball said, "Let's see what's left of the umbrella."

Eddie handed it to Mr. Cornball, who looked it over carefully. He saw that the cover was torn but told Eddie that the metal ribs were unharmed. "Just needs a new cover," he said.

"I don't know where to get one," said Eddie.

"Oh, my wife could cover it," said Mr. Cornball. "She could do a good job."

Eddie's face brightened. "She could!"

"You go over and see her," said Mr. Cornball. "We live just across the street. You go over and ring the bell for upstairs."

Eddie ran across the street. When he rang

the bell, the latch clicked and Eddie opened the door. He looked up the stairs and saw Mrs. Cornball in the upstairs hall. "Who's there?" Mrs. Cornball called down.

"It's me, Eddie Wilson," Eddie called back. "You remember I bought that hat like Mr. Cornball's."

"I remember you well," Mrs. Cornball replied. "Come up."

Eddie climbed the stairs, and Mrs. Cornball motioned him into a neat living room. He held up the tattered umbrella and said, "Mr. Cornball says you can put a new cover on this."

"I guess I can," said Mrs. Cornball, "but I don't know whether I have enough material in the same color for the job."

"Oh, Mrs. Cornball, I have to get it covered!" Eddie exclaimed. "You see, the girl that owns this umbrella has my hat, and she won't give it back to me until I give her a good umbrella."

Mrs. Cornball was very sympathetic. "Well, I'll look in my fabric box and see what I have," she said.

Mrs. Cornball brought out a large cardboard box and lifted the lid. The box was full of pieces of red, white, and blue material. She held them up one at a time, and each time she said, "Not enough to cover an umbrella."

When she was putting the lid back on the box, Eddie said, "Look, Mrs. Cornball, what about making Gloria a red, white, and blue umbrella like my hat?"

"Why, Eddie," Mrs. Cornball exclaimed, "I think I could do that! But will the girl like it?"

"Like it!" exclaimed Eddie. "I think she'll be crazy about it."

"I'll do it," said Mrs. Cornball. "It's a good idea. If it turns out well, I'll make some others to sell."

"How much will it cost, Mrs. Cornball?" Eddie asked.

"You've given me such a good idea I'll make this first one for nothing."

"Oh, Mrs. Cornball," Eddie cried, throwing his arms around her neck. "That's wonderful!"

"I'll let you have it in a week," said Mrs. Cornball.

Gloria wore Eddie's hat to school every day. She acted as though it were her very own.

At the end of the week, Eddie went to Mrs. Cornball to pick up the umbrella. When he saw it he was delighted. Like his hat, it was made of pie-shaped pieces that were red, white, and blue.

The following morning Eddie took the umbrella to school. When Gloria arrived, Eddie opened the umbrella and said, "Here's your umbrella, Gloria!"

"Oh, Eddie!" Gloria cried. "That's the most beautiful umbrella I ever saw in my life. It's even more beautiful than your hat."

"Well, give me my hat," said Eddie.

Gloria handed the hat to Eddie and said, "Just one thing. This umbrella doesn't have my name on it."

"That's because it might wash off in the rain," said Eddie.

"Oh, Eddie," said Gloria. "You always get the last word." Then Eddie and Gloria laughed and walked away with their red, white, and blue treasures.

Chapter 6

GLORIA'S CINDY

ONE DAY GLORIA spent the whole of her lunch period talking to Eddie about her cat, Cindy. "You should see my Cindy! She's the most beautiful cat you ever saw."

"There are some beauties at the pet shop," said Eddie.

"I bought Cindy at the pet shop a long time ago," said Gloria. "She was such a cute kitten. The reason I named her Cindy is because she's all black with just two white paws and a smudge of white on her nose."

"Smudges are black, not white," said Eddie.

"That's what you think," said Gloria. "Smudges can be any color. A smudge can be green."

Just then Sylvia came along. "What's green?" she said. "Green's my favorite color."

"Gloria has a cat with a green smudge on its nose," said Eddie.

"No, no!" said Gloria. "It's a white smudge."

"Who ever heard of a white smudge?" said Sylvia.

Eddie laughed. "Didn't I tell you, Gloria. Smudges are never white."

"Well, if you ran into some fresh white paint, you might get a white smudge on that hat," said Gloria.

"OK, so your cat has a white smudge on its nose," said Eddie.

"That's right," said Gloria, pleased that she had for once put Eddie down.

The following day Gloria brought pictures of Cindy to show to Eddie. "See, Eddie," she said, "isn't Cindy the most beautiful cat you ever saw? And look at the white smudge on her nose?"

Eddie took the pictures in his hands and said, "She sure is a beautiful cat."

One day Gloria called Eddie on the telephone. She sounded very upset as she said, "Oh, Eddie, something's the matter with my Cindy. Could you come over to my house? My mother's out, and I don't know what to do. Please, can you come over?"

"Sure," Eddie replied, "I'll be right over. Don't worry about her." Eddie felt that a real vet would say, "Don't worry about her." After all, if he was going to be a vet when he grew up, he couldn't begin too soon to talk like one.

Eddie got on his bicycle and pedaled over to Gloria's house. When he arrived he found her sitting with Cindy on her lap. "Oh, Eddie," she said, "I'm so glad you came. I don't know what is the matter with Cindy. She won't eat anything, not even milk, and she's so droopy."

Eddie picked up the cat. He looked her over, and finally he said, "She's all swollen. I think if Mr. Cornball could see her, he might know what's the matter with her."

"But will Mr. Cornball know what to do for her?" Gloria asked.

"He might," said Eddie. "He's real smart with animals. How about if we take Cindy over to Mr. Cornball?"

"All right," said Gloria, "but I can't ride my bike and carry Cindy."

"I have a basket on my bike," said Eddie. "I'll put her in the basket."

"Oh, not without a cushion," said Gloria.

"I'll get the cushion out of Cindy's cat basket."

Cindy was soon made comfortable in Eddie's basket, and the children started for the pet shop.

When they arrived, Eddie said to Gloria, "You take her to the stable. I'm sure Mr. Cornball wouldn't want us to bring a sick cat into the pet shop. I'll go in and ask him to come out."

"All right," said Gloria. "Be quick, Eddie."

While Gloria carried Cindy to the stable Eddie went into the shop. Mr. Cornball was right there. "Hello, Eddie!" he said. "What can I do for you?"

"Oh, Mr. Cornball," said Eddie, "my friend Gloria is out in the stable with her cat, Cindy. Cindy seems very sick, and I thought you might take a look at her."

"Of course, I'll take a look at her," said Mr. Cornball. "But you know I'm not a vet, so I don't know if I can do anything for her."

"I hope you can, Mr. Cornball," said Eddie,

"because Cindy means an awful lot to Gloria."

"Of course, of course," said Mr. Cornball, as he led the way to the stable.

They found Gloria sitting on a bench holding Cindy in her arms and murmuring, "It's all right, Cindy. Mr. Cornball will make you better."

Mr. Cornball took Cindy from Gloria. He held her gently as he examined her while the children stood by him looking very worried.

"Tut, tut," Mr. Cornball said. "I don't like the look of this. I'm afraid she's been poisoned."

"Poisoned?" exclaimed Gloria. "Who would poison my Cindy?"

"Never can tell," said Mr. Cornball. "Some people just don't like cats."

"I can't believe anyone would poison Cindy," said Eddie.

"Oh, Mr. Cornball," Gloria replied with tears in her eyes, "you can fix her, can't you?"

Mr. Cornball looked down at Cindy, and

then he looked at the children. They all heard Cindy sigh and saw her tremble. Then Mr. Cornball said, "I'm sorry, but it's all over with Cindy."

"No, no!" Gloria cried. "My Cindy can't die! She can't!"

Mr. Cornball put his hand on Gloria's head and patted her. "There, there, don't cry, little one."

Tears were rolling out of Eddie's eyes too. "I know how you feel, Gloria," he said. "I've lost pets too, so I know how you feel."

Gloria looked up at Mr. Cornball and said, "What will you do with her now?"

"I'll get a plastic bag," said Mr. Cornball, and he laid Cindy down on the bench. "I'll be right back."

Mr. Cornball left the weeping children looking down at Cindy. Gloria patted her as her tears fell on Cindy's fur.

When Mr. Cornball came back, he picked

up Cindy and was about to put her into the bag.

But suddenly Gloria cried out, "Oh, no, no! That's a garbage bag! My Cindy isn't garbage. Don't you dare put my Cindy in the garbage."

"I'm not going to put her in the garbage," said Mr. Cornball. "I'll take her out into a nice woods and bury her."

"Not in a garbage bag," said Gloria.

"Well, what do you want?" asked Mr. Cornball very gently.

"I want her wrapped up in something nice," said Gloria.

"I'm afraid I don't have anything nicer than this," said Mr. Cornball.

"You wait," said Eddie. "I'll go home, and my mother will find something."

As he got on his bicycle, Eddie said, "I won't be long, I'll be right back."

When Eddie reached home, he said to his mother, "Oh, Ma, something terrible happened.

Gloria's beautiful cat, Cindy, is dead. Mr. Cornball said she was poisoned. I think she may have gone into someone's garbage can and eaten food that was bad for her."

"That *is* dreadful," his mother agreed. "Where is Gloria now?"

"Over at Mr. Cornball's," said Eddie. "He was going to put Cindy into a plastic bag, but Gloria won't have it. She wants Cindy wrapped up in something nice."

"I see," said Eddie's mother. "So you've come home for something nice?"

"That's right, Ma," said Eddie. "Do you think you could find something nice to wrap Cindy in?"

"I'll go see," his mother replied, as she started up the stairs.

Eddie waited. He could hear his mother opening closets and pulling out drawers from the chest in the hall.

When she came down, Eddie saw she had something that was pale blue over her arm. "How would this be?" she said. "It's a lovely old bath towel. It's old because it was one of my wedding presents, but it's still pretty. See, it has my initial on it, a big *C* for Catherine."

"I think that's great, Ma," said Eddie. "I think Gloria will be pleased. Thanks a million."

Mrs. Wilson handed the towel to Eddie. Then she leaned over and wiped a tear off his cheek. She kissed him and said, "Tell Gloria I'm sorry. I had a precious cat die when I was a little girl."

"Did you cry, Ma?" Eddie asked.

"Indeed I did cry," Mrs. Wilson replied.

Eddie placed the towel in the basket on his bicycle and started back to Mr. Cornball's stable. When he arrived, he handed the towel to Gloria and said, "Do you like this, Gloria?"

"Oh, it's beautiful! It's beautiful!" said Gloria.

"It was one of my mother's wedding presents," said Eddie.

"That's wonderful," said Gloria, examining the towel. Suddenly she said, "Oh, it has a big *C* embroidered on it."

"Yes," said Eddie, "my mother's name is Catherine."

Gloria looked up at Mr. Cornball and said, "Isn't it lovely, 'cause *C* is for Cindy too?"

"Certainly is," said Mr. Cornball, taking the towel from Gloria.

Then the children watched him wrap Cindy in the blue towel. He did it carefully so that the embroidered *C* was right on the top of Cindy. "Now I'll find a nice place to bury her," he said. "You better go home and don't cry anymore. Cindy is where all good cats go."

Gloria and Eddie got on their bicycles and started for home. When they parted at Gloria's front gate, Gloria said, "Mr. Cornball is a nice man, isn't he?"

"He's great," said Eddie. "First time I went into his shop I thought he was an old sourpuss, but now I know him I think he's just great."

Several weeks later, on a Saturday morning, Eddie arrived early at the pet shop. When he looked into the window he was surprised to see three new kittens: two gray ones and a black one with white paws. "Why, Mr. Cornball," said Eddie, "I see there are three new kittens."

"Nice ones," said Mr. Cornball. "A woman brought them in yesterday. Said her cat had a litter three weeks ago. She gave two away, but can't find a home for these three. I offered to pay for them, but she said she was happy to get rid of them."

Eddie reached into the window and picked up the black kitten. "You know what?" he said. "This kitten looks a lot like Gloria's Cindy. It even has white paws."

Mr. Cornball looked at the kitten. "You're

right, Eddie," he said. "Certainly does resemble Cindy."

"Has everything except the white smudge that Cindy had on her nose," said Eddie.

"Tell you what, Eddie," said Mr. Cornball. "Why don't you take that kitten to Gloria? It will make her feel better about losing Cindy."

"Oh, Mr. Cornball!" exclaimed Eddie. "You mean you'll give this kitten to Gloria?"

"That's right," said Mr. Cornball.

"But you could sell it," said Eddie. "Probably get a good price for it."

"I got it for nothing," said Mr. Cornball, "and if I want to give it away, why shouldn't I?"

"It's very kind of you," said Eddie, "and the kitten will make Gloria happy, 'cause she misses her Cindy."

"Well, you take it to her," said Mr. Cornball.

"Tell you what I'll do," said Eddie. "I'll take

the kitten home with me, and early tomorrow morning I'll go over to Gloria's and open the door of their back porch and put the kitten on the porch. When Gloria gets up, she'll find a big surprise."

"Good idea," said Mr. Cornball.

At the end of the morning, when Eddie left the shop, he took the kitten with him. Eddie decided that he would introduce the dogs to the kitten to avoid any trouble, so he took the dogs one by one to the kitten's basket in the kitchen. Patsy was the first to be introduced. She took one look at the kitten and barked furiously. Fritz was the next, and he poked his nose into the basket and began licking the kitten. When Hippie arrived, he didn't even look at the kitten but went to the dish of milk and licked it clean.

Suddenly the kitten jumped out of the basket and landed right on top of Hippie, who paid no more attention to the kitten than if it had been a fly. Finally the kitten jumped to the floor and went to the milk dish. When it found the dish empty, it sat down beside Eddie and began to cry. Eddie poured some more milk into the empty dish, and the kitten ran to it, beating Hippie to the milk. Hippie decided to eat his dinner as did Fritz and Patsy. All of the animals went to bed happy.

On Sunday morning Eddie got up early and carried the kitten to Gloria's house. He went to the back of the house and quietly opened the door of the back porch. Then he placed the kitten inside and went home.

Early in the afternoon the telephone rang. Eddie picked up the receiver. "That you, Eddie?" Gloria's voice asked.

"Hi, Gloria," said Eddie.

"Oh, Eddie," said Gloria, "the most wonderful thing has happened to me."

"What happened?" Eddie asked.

"My mother opened the back door this morning, and you'll never guess, but there on the back porch was an adorable black kitten. It looks just the way my Cindy looked when she was a kitten. It even has white paws."

"Does it have a white smudge on its nose?" Eddie asked.

"No," Gloria replied, "but that doesn't matter. Where do you suppose it came from?"

"You never can tell about kittens," said Eddie.

"Do you think Mr. Cornball could have put the kitten on our porch?" Gloria asked.

"You never can tell about Mr. Cornball," said Eddie. "He's a mighty nice man, and I bet he wouldn't tell."

"Were you at the pet shop yesterday?" Gloria asked.

"Sure, I work there every Saturday," Eddie replied.

"I bet you had something to do with this kitten," said Gloria. "I just bet you did."

"Oh, go on," said Eddie. "I have to hang up and feed my dogs."

Before Gloria hung up, she said, "Mr. Cornball is a nice man, Eddie, and you're nice too."

Chapter 7

SANDY LOVICKI COMES
TO THE FAIR

Now EDDIE WAS LOOKING forward to the annual Spring Fair. It was held for the benefit of the local hospital on the parking lot at the railroad station under a large tent. Outside the tent there would be a Ferris wheel, which Eddie always enjoyed riding on. But the thing that Eddie was looking forward to the most was meeting a college baseball player named Sandy Lovicki.

Sandy Lovicki was a friend of Eddie's teacher, Mr. Jeffrey, who was a member of the committee in charge of the Fair. Mr. Jeffrey had persuaded Sandy Lovicki to attend the Fair, for he was sure that the ballplayer's presence would attract a big crowd. Sandy Lovicki had made a name for himself pitching for Spencer University, which was located in a town about sixty miles away. His picture had been in all the local papers and even in some magazines, and supposedly both the Phillies and the Boston Red Sox were watching him. His record included several recent no-hit games for his team.

As the day for the Fair drew near Eddie's excitement over the thought of seeing this remarkable baseball player grew. "Imagine meeting Sandy Lovicki," Eddie said to his brothers.

"You won't be meeting him," said Joe. "You'll be lucky if you see him."

"Sure I'll meet him," said Eddie. "He'll shake my hand. Just think! He'll shake my hand with the same hand that holds the balls he pitches! I'll never wash my hand again!"

"That's what you think," said his mother, who was standing by.

There were other things Eddie was looking forward to at the Fair. There would be pony-cart rides, with Punky and Gramp. I mustn't forget an apple for Punky, thought Eddie. There would be bagpipes playing and lots of good things to eat: big wads of cotton candy, soft drinks, thick turkey sandwiches, and hot dogs.

One of the most popular features of the Fair was the used-clothing booth called Monkey Business. Many residents of the town gave expensive clothes to be sold at the Fair and the clothes were always clean and in good condi-

tion. Mrs. Wilson was one of the volunteers who ran the Monkey Business booth, so she was always very busy the day of the Fair. The Monkey Business booth was so popular that people lined up long before the Fair opened at nine o'clock. Sometimes the line was two blocks long, and people were known to arrive as early as six o'clock.

There were also booths that sold books, flowers, jams and jellies, and fancy goods like Mrs. Cornball's. Eddie wondered whether Mrs. Cornball would have a booth like the one she had at the County Fair. Perhaps she would be selling red, white, and blue umbrellas.

Still another specialty was the furniture auction, which always raised a lot of money for the hospital.

Mr. Cornball told Eddie and Rudy to take the morning off to go to the Fair as it was held on a Saturday. So, when the day arrived, Eddie and his brothers got to the Fair as soon as it opened. They wanted to be there when the baseball hero arrived. Most of the boys and girls were looking forward to welcoming Sandy Lovicki.

He was due to arrive by train at the railroad station at ten o'clock in the morning. Well before the hour, the station platform was crowded with Sandy Lovicki's fans. Eddie, wearing his hat, was in the midst of the crowd, and Mr. Jeffrey, the tallest man around, was there too, waiting to welcome his friend.

When the train whistle sounded the whole crowd shouted, "Here it comes!" Eddie's face grew hot and his hands cold. He was about to see Sandy Lovicki in the flesh.

The train squealed to a stop. Then the door opened, and a man appeared. Everyone who had seen his photograph in the newspapers recognized Sandy Lovicki. Mr. Jeffrey made his way forward to greet the ballplayer.

"Hurrah! Hurrah!" the crowd shouted. "Hurrah for Sandy Lovicki!"

With a big smile the ballplayer waved his arm and called out, "Hi, everybody! Just call me Sandy!"

"Hi, Sandy!" the boys and girls replied.

Sandy stood beside Mr. Jeffrey, looking at this gathering of his fans. Then to Eddie's great surprise, Sandy called out, "Say, you in that hat! Can you push through? I want to see you up here."

Eddie looked around to see if anyone else was wearing a hat, but he seemed to be the only one. So he decided that Sandy Lovicki was speaking to him. Making his way through the crowd, Eddie soon found himself standing in front of the ballplayer.

Sandy shook Eddie's hand and, touching the visor on Eddie's hat, said, "I see you're Eddie. Well, Eddie, that's a great hat! Where did you buy it?"

"I'm glad you like it," said Eddie. "I bought it from Mrs. Cornball. She made it."

"Like it!" said Sandy. "I'm crazy about it. Do you think I could get one for myself?"

"I think Mrs. Cornball has a booth here at the Fair," said Eddie. "Maybe she has another hat."

"Lead me to Mrs. Cornball," said Sandy.

The crowd gave way for Eddie and Sandy so they could get to the tent. As soon as they entered, Eddie could see Mrs. Cornball's booth. It was decorated with red, white, and blue umbrellas and hats like Eddie's.

"It's right over there," said Eddie, pointing to the booth.

When they reached it, Eddie said to Mrs. Cornball, "This is Sandy Lovicki, Mrs. Cornball. He's the Spencer University baseball player."

"Indeed, we all know Sandy Lovicki," said

Mrs. Cornball, "and we're honored to have you here today."

"Well, Mrs. Cornball," said Sandy, "if you have a hat like Eddie's that would fit me, I would like to buy it."

"You're welcome to try them on," said Mrs. Cornball.

Eddie watched Sandy try on several hats. Soon he found one that fitted him and bought it.

"I'm sorry it doesn't have your name on it," said Mrs. Cornball. "If I had known you were interested in a hat, I would have put your name on the visor."

"It's fine just as it is," said Sandy.

"Sure," said Eddie, "you don't need to have your name on the visor. Everyone knows who you are."

Sandy walked off in his new hat and joined Mr. Jeffrey and the rest of the committeemen in charge of the Fair. They went outside the tent where a shuffleboard game had been laid out. Soon Eddie and Jimmie went out to see how the game was coming along. They found that photographers from the local newspapers had arrived, which stopped the shuffleboard game. Sandy Lovicki was photographed alone and then with Mr. Jeffrey. Then he was photographed with the whole committee.

More children had arrived and were watching the photographers. One of the photographers called to them and said, "Come on, kids, get in the picture!" All of the children together with Eddie and Jimmie ran to be photographed with Sandy Lovicki. When the group was arranged to suit the photographer, he said to them, "Now give us a big smile. Say 'cheese.'"

Eddie sneezed. Everyone laughed.

"Too bad," said the photographer. "Let's try it again. Stop wriggling."

The children straightened up, and once again Eddie sneezed.

"Do you do that all the time?" said the photographer. "I'm using up my film. Now let's try it again. Say 'cheese.'"

This time Eddie did not sneeze, but he was embarrassed to have ruined two photographs. He said to Sandy Lovicki, "I'm sorry I spoiled the pictures."

"Don't worry about that, Eddie," said Sandy. "I'm sure most of them are going to be OK, and we'll all see ourselves in the newspaper."

Then Sandy Lovicki gave a pitching exhibition after which he spent a long time signing autographs for the children.

The next time Eddie saw Sandy Lovicki he was standing with a group of people in front of the furniture auction platform.

Eddie saw that Jimmie's father was the auctioneer, and he heard Jimmie's father asking for bids on a child's highchair.

"What am I bid on this fine highchair? Genuine antique! I want a good bid," called out Jimmie's father.

Eddie was surprised to see that the highchair was his old one. It had been in the Wilsons' attic ever since Eddie had outgrown it. Evidently his mother had decided to donate it for the furniture sale.

Eddie was surprised again when he heard someone offer two dollars for the chair. It seemed very little to him. But the price began to go up, and then Eddie heard a familiar voice call out "Twelve dollars." It was Sandy Lovicki.

Jimmie's father heard him too, and he called out, "Twelve dollars. Do I hear thirteen?"

Jimmie's father did not hear thirteen, so he said, "Twelve dollars once, twelve dollars twice, going for twelve dollars." Then he cried, "Sold for twelve dollars to Sandy Lovicki."

Sandy Lovicki handed the twelve dollars to

Jimmie's father, and as he walked away Eddie caught up with him. "That was my highchair you just bought," he said.

"Well, imagine that," said Sandy Lovicki. "Now my little brother Peetie will be sitting in Eddie's highchair."

"I hope he'll like it," said Eddie.

"Oh, he'll like it," said Sandy, "if I can ever get it home. I can't carry it home on the train. I should have thought of that before I bought it, but it's such a nice highchair I felt I had to have it."

"Just wait a minute," said Eddie. "I thought of something. I think I can fix it. I'll be back in a minute."

Eddie ran off to look for his father. He found him managing the record player that played music over the loudspeaker. "Oh, Dad," said Eddie. "Guess what? Sandy Lovicki bought my highchair for his little brother Peetie. Just think of that! Sandy Lovicki's little brother sitting in my highchair. That's something."

Jimmie, who was standing by, said, "Gee, it isn't a throne. It's just a highchair. Of course, when Peetie grows up, maybe he'll be a ball-player like his brother. Then you can go around saying, 'Just think, Peetie Lovicki sat in my highchair.'"

Eddie paid no attention to Jimmie but went on speaking to his father. "Dad," he said, "couldn't we drive the highchair in our station wagon to Sandy Lovicki's house? It's only about sixty miles. Sandy can't take it on the train."

"Sure, we'll take it," said his father.

Eddie ran back to Sandy Lovicki and said, "It's all fixed, Sandy. Dad says we'll bring the highchair to your house in our station wagon. I'll let you know when."

"That's great," said Sandy Lovicki. "You're a swell fixer, Eddie."

Eddie laughed. "I sure fixed those photographs."

"Forget it," said Sandy. "It's time for lunch. I'll see you later."

Eddie and his brothers ate their sandwiches with Jimmie while Sandy Lovicki had his lunch with Mr. Jeffrey and the committee.

After lunch Eddie went to the stand where cotton candy was sold. There he found Sandy Lovicki and Mr. Jeffrey eating cotton candy. Sandy said to him, "Here's Eddie again. Come on, let's take a ride on the Ferris wheel."

Eddie could hardly believe he had been invited for a ride by Sandy Lovicki, but he followed Sandy to the Ferris wheel and sat down beside him.

"Now," said Sandy Lovicki to Eddie, "tell me about yourself, Eddie. Do you have any hobbies?"

"Oh, sure," said Eddie. "I have hobbies."

"Like what?" said Sandy.

"Animals are one of my hobbies," said Eddie, "and I collect valuable property."

"I know what animals are," said Sandy, "but what is 'valuable property'?"

Eddie laughed. "My dad calls it junk, but I call it valuable property."

Sandy pulled his pitcher's glove out of his coat pocket and held it up. "How about this?" he said. "It's an old one, but would you call this valuable property?"

"Oh, boy," Eddie cried, "would I call that valuable property! It sure is."

"Would you like to have it?" Sandy asked.

"Oh, would I!" said Eddie.

"Well, it's yours," said Sandy, giving the glove to Eddie.

Eddie took it in his hands. "Oh, thanks," he said. "Thanks a million."

Eddie put his hand into the glove. "Just think," he said, "you must have put your hand in this glove a lot of times."

"It's had a good workout," said Sandy.

"Would you mind autographing it for me?" said Eddie.

"Glad to," said Sandy, taking a pen out of his breast pocket.

Eddie watched Sandy as he wrote his name on the glove. "That's great," said Eddie, as Sandy handed the glove back to him. "I never thought I'd know a ballplayer like you."

"What do you want to be when you grow up?" Sandy asked, as the Ferris wheel began to move.

"I'm going to be a vet," said Eddie.

"How come?" Sandy asked.

Then Eddie told him all about the pet shop and how he was the volunteer watcher-outer for shoplifters.

"I guess you're a good watcher-outer," said Sandy.

"You bet I am," said Eddie.

When the Ferris wheel stopped, Sandy said,

"I guess it's about time for me to get my train. This has been a great ride, Eddie, and I'm sure glad to know you." Eddie felt warm all over.

Eddie and a large crowd of children followed Sandy to the train that was waiting at the station. Mr. Jeffrey took Sandy to the door of the train while the crowd on the station platform shouted, "Hurrah for Sandy Lovicki! Good-bye, Sandy!"

Sandy Lovicki waved to the crowd and shouted, "Good-bye! Good-bye, everybody!"

The Wilson boys waited with the crowd until the train moved out of the station. Then they went to find the family car, for Mr. Wilson was going to drive home at five o'clock.

When they reached the car, the four boys climbed into the back. Eddie showed his brothers Sandy Lovicki's glove.

"You mean he gave it to you for keeps!" exclaimed Joe.

"Yep," said Eddie.

"I don't know why you're so lucky," said Frank, as he examined the glove.

"Maybe it's that hat," said Rudy. "It brings him good luck."

Eddie laughed and said, "Well, I'm certainly lucky to have Sandy's glove, and I'm going to take good care of it."

His three brothers all put their hands into the glove. "Just imagine," said Joe, "Sandy Lovicki's glove!"

When the boys reached home, Eddie showed the glove to his mother, who was already there. "Just think, Ma, Sandy Lovicki's hand was in this glove," he said.

"What's so wonderful about that?" said his mother. "I can give you an old glove that my hand has been in."

"Oh, Ma," said Eddie, "you don't understand. This glove has been on the hand of a star ballplayer. His hand is special. Maybe it's even insured. 'Magine having an insured hand."

"Well, go wash yours that isn't insured," said his mother. "Dinner is ready."

"OK," said Eddie, and he ran upstairs to his room. He placed the glove very tenderly on the chair beside his bed. Then he ran to the bathroom and washed his hands.

After dinner, he worked on his homework for Monday.

At half past nine he went up to his room. When he walked in, his eyes immediately went to the chair beside his bed. The glove was not there. Eddie looked on the floor. It was strewn with bits and pieces of material. Eddie picked up one of the pieces. He could see at once that it was part of Sandy Lovicki's glove.

Eddie let out a scream that brought Rudy flying up the stairs. "Eddie," he said, "what's the matter with you?"

"Oh, look," Eddie cried, "Sandy Lovicki's glove is all torn up. One of those dogs must have torn it up." Eddie was on his hands and knees trying to put the pieces together as though it were a jigsaw puzzle.

"That's too bad," said Rudy.

"It was probably Hippie's work. He was a great one for chewing things up when he was a puppy," said Eddie.

"He should get a good thrashing," said Rudy, "but you're so soft on those dogs you'll probably pat him on the head and say, 'He's just a dog'."

"Well, it might have been Fritz," said Eddie. "I wouldn't want to beat the wrong dog."

"Oh, no," said Rudy, "just give them something extra in their dish tomorrow."

Eddie went to bed feeling very sad, but at least he could stretch his legs all the way down to the bottom of the bed. As punishment he had locked the dogs out of the room, and they were lying outside of Eddie's door. Every once in a while one of them cried to get in, but Eddie stayed in his snug bed.

Chapter 8

THE CLUB

ON THE FOLLOWING MONDAY morning, when Eddie reached school and saw his class lined up in the yard, so many boys were wearing red, white, and blue hats that there seemed to be a Fourth of July parade in progress.

A few minutes before the bell sounded, Gloria ran up and got behind him. "See," she said, "I finally got a hat like yours. Isn't it terrific?"

"Sure!" Eddie replied. "But it's a boy's hat. Not for girls."

"It is if a girl wants to wear it," said Gloria. "But do you know what?"

"What?" said Eddie.

"I think we should form a club," said Gloria. "Everybody who has one of these hats could be in the club. Hats and clubs go together you know."

"What do you mean 'they go together'?" said Eddie.

"Well," said Gloria, "my father belongs to a club, and all of the members wear hats. My father has one with a tassel on it."

Just then the bell rang, and the fifth-grade line began to move. When the boys and girls reached their room, the boys took off their hats but Gloria kept hers on. She continued talking to Eddie. "A club is just the thing," she said. "I think a good name for the club would be the Sandy Lovicki Club, because we all have Sandy Lovicki hats."

"I thought it was an Eddie Wilson hat," said Eddie, "but it's OK with me if now it's a Sandy Lovicki hat."

"Now what about this club?" said Gloria. "It would be nice to hold our meetings in your barn."

"What would we do at our meetings?" Eddie asked.

"We could talk about Sandy Lovicki and eat," Gloria said.

"Eat!" said Eddie. "What?"

"Oh, cookies and hot chocolate would be nice," said Gloria.

"Great!" said Eddie. "Let's have the meetings at your house."

"All right," said Gloria, "but you'll be sorry

because I'm going to invite Sandy Lovicki to the first meeting of the club. I bet you'd like Sandy Lovicki to come to your barn."

"He won't come," said Eddie. "Do you think a baseball player like Sandy Lovicki is going to take time to fool around with a bunch of kids?"

"You just wait and see," said Gloria.

Gloria lost no time in spreading the news that she was organizing a Sandy Lovicki Club. "Only kids who have Sandy Lovicki hats can join," she said. No one seemed anxious to join until she said, "I'm going to ask Sandy Lovicki to come to our first meeting."

Now everyone wanted to join the club. By the end of the day there were twelve members.

On Saturday Mrs. Cornball told Eddie that she had so many orders for hats that she had to buy more red, white, and blue material. Soon there were so many hats in Eddie's class that they kept getting mixed up. From time to time, voices rose in argument.

One would say, "That's my hat you have."

Another would answer, "No, this is my hat. Jimmie has your hat."

Then Jimmie would say, "What d' ya mean? Don't you think I know my own hat?"

Eddie's hat was the only one that didn't get lost.

Mr. Jeffrey got so tired of hearing about mixed-up hats that he finally said, "Look, Eddie's hat has his name on the visor. You should all have your names on the visors too. I have some white paint that can be used on fabric. Before we do anything else today I want you to paint your name on the visor of your hat."

Everyone liked the idea, but there were some who said, "I can't make letters that are nice enough to go on my hat."

"I can make good letters," said Eddie. "If anybody can't do his hat, I'll do it for him."

Mr. Jeffrey put the white paint and some brushes on the worktable.

Gloria stepped up to the table. "Here, Eddie," she said. "You do it for me."

Eddie picked up a brush and dipped it in the white paint. Gloria watched Eddie begin with *G*. He followed it with *L O R I*, and then he made an *O*.

"Eddie!" Gloria cried. "You made an *O* instead of an *A*."

"Well, it's a nice *O*," said Eddie. "I think Glorio is a good name."

Gloria looked at her visor and said, "Oh, dear, I guess it will have to stay that way."

Jimmie came forward with his hat. "Now do it right, Eddie," he said.

"I'll do it right," said Eddie, as he dipped his brush into the paint. Eddie set to work, but when he had finished he had left out one of the *M*'s.

"Now look what you did," said Jimmie. "You left out an *M*."

Mr. Jeffrey looked at the hat and said, "Now you're Jimie."

The children laughed. Larry called out, "Jimie, do you like jime on your bread?"

A boy named Peter was the next to bring his hat to Eddie. "Now get it right, Eddie," said Peter.

"Don't worry," said Eddie, as he set to work.

Suddenly Peter cried out, "You drew two *T*'s instead of one. I'm not Petter, I'm Peter."

"Eddie," said Mr. Jeffrey, "you make nice letters, but you better let me take over the job before you change the names of everyone in the class."

Gloria was already being called Glorio. Jimmie was called Jimie, and Peter was Petter.

"I'm glad, Mr. Jeffrey," said Larry, " 'cause Eddie would probably leave out one of the *R*'s in my name." He handed his hat to Mr. Jeffrey,

but just as he was about to make the letter *L*, he upset the bottle of paint. The paint ran across the visor of Larry's hat.

"What a mess!" exclaimed Mr. Jeffrey. "I guess I'll have to paint your visor white. I'm sorry, but I think it will be all right. I can paint your name with blue paint."

"OK," said Larry. "I'll be different."

By the end of the morning every visor displayed the name of the hat's owner and no one was calling out, "You've got my hat."

One morning Gloria said to Eddie, "I wrote to Sandy Lovicki and invited him to come to our first club meeting, but I haven't heard anything from him yet."

"He won't come," said Eddie.

"Maybe he will," said Gloria.

When the rest of the children learned that Gloria had invited Sandy Lovicki, they kept asking about him. "Have you heard from Sandy

Lovicki?" they would say. The days passed, however, and there was no reply to Gloria's letter.

"See," said Eddie one day, "he isn't even going to answer your letter."

Gloria went on waiting and hoping, and at last the day came when a letter from Sandy Lovicki arrived. He said he felt honored to have a club named for him, but he was sorry he could not come to the first meeting. Then he said, "Spencer is playing a championship game against Grant University here on our field next month. I'm inviting everyone who has a hat to come to the game."

Gloria could hardly wait to get to school with the letter. When she showed it to Eddie, he said, "Boy, that's the greatest!"

When Mr. Jeffrey heard the news, he said he would take the children by bus to the game.

The members of the Sandy Lovicki Club were thrilled with Gloria's news, but Roland was very unhappy. Roland was not a member of the club, because he didn't have a Sandy Lovicki hat. It was too expensive for him to buy.

Eddie felt sorry about Roland, and he began to wonder how he could get a hat for Roland to wear to the game. One day, when Mr. Cornball was wearing his hat in the pet shop, Eddie had an idea. "Mr. Cornball," he said, "Sandy Lovicki has invited our Sandy Lovicki Club to attend the championship game in which he'll be pitching against Grant University."

"Isn't that great," said Mr. Cornball.

"Yes," said Eddie, "but my friend Roland can't go."

"That's too bad," said Mr. Cornball. "Why can't he go?"

"Because he doesn't have any hat," said Eddie.

"That's hard luck," said Mr. Cornball.

Eddie hesitated. Then he said, "Uh, uh—"

"Yes, Eddie," said Mr. Cornball. "What's on your mind?"

"Well, uh," said Eddie, "I was thinking, would you mind lending Roland your hat so he could go to the game?"

"Of course, I'll lend Roland my hat," said Mr. Cornball.

Eddie jumped up and down with pleasure. "You will! That's wonderful. Yippie!"

All of the puppies began to cry "Yippie!"

Eddie could hardly wait to tell Roland the good news. Roland, of course, was delighted. "I'll take good care of the hat," he said.

"I know you will," said Eddie.

The day before the bus trip, Mr. Cornball gave his hat to Eddie and Eddie went over to Roland's house with it. "Here's the hat," said Eddie, and he slapped it on Roland's head.

Roland's head disappeared inside the hat. The visor came down over his eyes and nose. "I can't see! I can't see!" Roland cried.

Eddie adjusted the hat so the visor hung in the back against Roland's collar. "That will be all right," said Eddie.

"It's a funny way to wear a hat," said Roland.

"Don't be so fussy," said Eddie. "You've got a hat, and now you can go to the game."

Saturday was the big day, so Eddie had the morning off from the pet shop. The club members gathered with Mr. Jeffrey outside the school for the special bus to take them to the game. Everyone was wearing his hat including Roland, who had Mr. Cornball's hat hanging on the back of his head. It didn't look very secure, but Roland was delighted to be part of the crowd.

The children enjoyed the bus trip and sang most of the way.

When they reached the ball field, Mr. Jeffrey said to them, "Now keep right behind me. I don't want to lose any of you in this crowd."

It was indeed a crowd. Everyone seemed to have come for this important game. Mr. Jeffrey and the children followed the crowd through the entrance. Eddie looked around. He saw people swarming all over the grandstand, looking for their seat. There was a man selling hot dogs, and Eddie could hardly wait to buy one.

Mr. Jeffrey looked at the grandstand and said, "I know Sandy has reserved good seats for us."

He started to lead the way, but Eddie stopped to buy a hot dog for himself and one for Roland. Nearly all the other children bought a hot dog too. At last they were ready to follow Mr. Jeffrey to their seats.

As they neared them two boys about Rudy's age pushed past. Eddie heard one of them say to the other, "Get an eyeful of those hats." Then one of the boys reached out and knocked Roland's hat off.

"Watch it, fella!" said Mr. Jeffrey.

Roland turned to go after his hat, but Mr. Jeffrey said, "Get it later, Roland. We must find our seats now. I don't want to lose you."

Soon Mr. Jeffrey found the seats that Sandy Lovicki had reserved for them. "We're here," he said. The seats were right in back of the dugout, and the children were delighted with them. Unfortunately, the two unfriendly boys were sitting behind them.

Roland handed his hot dog to Eddie and said, "Hold this for me, Eddie. I have to go find my hat." He was moving against the oncoming crowd, but he finally got his hat from a man who had picked it up.

Before Roland got back, Eddie grew tired of holding his hot dog so he put it down on the seat beside him. He became so interested in what was happening on the field that he didn't notice when Mr. Jeffrey sat down on the seat.

"Where's my hot dog?" Roland asked Eddie, when he returned.

"Oh!" cried Eddie. "Oh, Mr. Jeffrey, I'm afraid you're sitting on Roland's hot dog."

Mr. Jeffrey jumped up. He looked at the hot dog. It was smashed flat.

"Oh, Mr. Jeffrey," said Eddie, "I'm afraid you have mustard on the seat of your pants."

"Ha, ha!" cried the two boys, who were sitting behind Eddie and Roland.

"Here's my paper napkin," said Roland. "Maybe Eddie can wipe the mustard off."

Eddie did his best to clean the mustard off Mr. Jeffrey's trousers. "It doesn't look too bad," said Eddie.

From time to time during the game the two boys in the row behind made fun of the children's hats. "Take off those silly hats!" they cried.

Mr. Jeffrey signaled to the children to pay no attention.

The hat crowd cheered Sandy Lovicki's team when they came on the field, and so did the boys behind them. But they kept making remarks about the hats in front of them. Still, everyone cheered especially loud for Sandy Lovicki. Eddie heard the boys behind say to each other, "Sandy Lovicki is the greatest!" It was the only thing they said that Eddie could agree with.

The game was an exciting one, for both teams were in excellent form. Sandy Lovicki gave up only three hits, and the first time he came up to bat he walloped a long double. His fans cheered him and stamped their feet.

At the end of the seventh inning the score was tied three to three. Eddie's hands were as cold as ice as Sandy came up to bat. The pitcher for Grant wound up and let the ball fly. Sandy gave it a terrific crack, and the ball flew over the fence and out of the ball field. Sandy Lovicki had hit a home run.

Mr. Jeffrey and the children stood up and cheered, and so did the boys behind them. Eddie wondered what those boys would think if they knew that Sandy Lovicki had invited him and his friends to the game.

The ninth inning ended with the score five to three in favor of Spencer. They had won the championship, and Sandy Lovicki's fans were filled with delight.

The cheering went on for a long time. Then Eddie heard one of the boys behind him say, "Oh, look, here comes Sandy Lovicki." Eddie was surprised to see Sandy coming toward them.

Then the other boy behind him said, "What do ya know! He's got one of those crazy hats, just like these guys."

"Yeah," said the other boy. "It looks good on him. I wonder where you get those hats."

Sandy Lovicki heard what the two boys had said and shook hands with them. "So you like my hat," he said.

"Oh, it's great," said the boys in a chorus. "It's a great hat."

Eddie turned around and said, "We call them Sandy Lovicki hats."

"Wish I had one," answered the first boy. To Roland, he said, "Sorry, kid, I knocked your hat off. Hope it didn't hurt it."

"It's OK," said Roland.

Then the hat crowd followed Sandy Lovicki, who took them down to the dugout where they met all the players on his team.

When Eddie arrived home, he told his family that it had been the greatest day of his life. "I'm not sure," he said, "but maybe I'll be a baseball player instead of a vet."

"Better start practicing," said Rudy.

Chapter 9

DREAMY

ONE SATURDAY MORNING, when Eddie and Rudy arrived at the pet shop, Mr. Cornball called out, "Hi, boys! It's a great day!"

Eddie felt that Mr. Cornball was excited about something. "It's always a great day here at the shop, Mr. Cornball," said Eddie.

"Oh, Eddie," said Mr. Cornball, "wait until you see what I have out in the stable."

"Is it some great Dane puppies?" Eddie asked. He knew that Mr. Cornball was expecting a litter of them.

"Better than that," said Mr. Cornball.

"Some new rabbits?" Rudy asked.

"Rabbits, nothing," said Mr. Cornball. "You come out and see what I have."

The boys followed Mr. Cornball out of the back door of the shop, and he led the way to the stable. They hadn't taken many steps when Eddie saw the head of a horse hanging over the lower half of a Dutch door. "Oh, Mr. Cornball!" Eddie exclaimed. "You're going to shoe a horse. I've been waiting to see you shoe a horse."

"No, no," said Mr. Cornball. "This little filly has her shoes on."

Eddie was disappointed. "Why, Mr. Cornball," he said, "you promised to let me see you put the shoes on. Don't you remember? You promised."

"I know," said Mr. Cornball, "but this creature came with her shoes on."

Eddie felt better. "Where did she come from, and what is she doing here?" he asked.

"A woman named Mrs. Grayson brought her in this morning early," said Mr. Cornball, opening the door into the stable. "She wants to sell the horse and asked me if I could take care of the sale. I told her that horses were not exactly my line in a pet shop but I'd see what I could do."

"What a beautiful horse!" said Rudy. "A filly, did you say?"

"That's right," replied Mr. Cornball. "A nice little girl if I ever saw one."

Eddie thrilled at the sight of the animal. "She's the most beautiful horse I've ever seen," he said, patting her lovely face. "Oh, Rudy, I

wish we could have her. Do you think Dad would buy her?"

"I don't know," Rudy replied.

"After all," said Eddie, "we need a horse to pull the sleigh in the barn."

"It would be great," said Rudy, "but I imagine she's expensive."

"Two hundred dollars," said Mr. Cornball, "but that's a bargain for such a beautiful filly. She'll be nice to ride as well as to pull a sleigh."

"What shall we name her?" Eddie asked.

"Don't be so quick, Eddie," said Rudy. "She doesn't belong to us."

"But we could name her," said Eddie. "I think Maisie would be a good name."

"I think Dreamy would be nicer," said Rudy. "She's like a beautiful dream."

"OK," said Eddie, "Dreamy is good." Eddie stroked the filly's head and murmured, "Dreamy girl, you're beautiful." The horse returned Eddie's caress by rubbing her face against

Eddie's head. "She likes her name," said Eddie. "I think she knows that she is dreamy."

At the end of the morning, when the time came for the boys to leave the shop, they went back to the stable to say good-bye to Dreamy. Then they took the bus for home. They talked about Dreamy all the way.

"Oh, I do hope Dad will buy her," said Eddie.

"Now, Eddie," said Rudy, "don't start right off about Dreamy. Lead up to her gradually. The idea of a horse will be very new to Dad, and he'll have to take time to think it over. Two hundred dollars is a lot of money."

"That's right," said Eddie. "I'll be careful. I'll lead up to the subject slowly. I'll talk to Dad about the horse the way a president of a foreign country talks to the president of the United States when he wants to borrow a lot of money. I'll make believe I'm the president of

Tiddyhut and Dad is president of the United States."

"Where is Tiddyhut?" Rudy asked.

"Oh, it's one of those countries near the South Pole covered with snow and ice all the year round," said Eddie. "A lot of penguins live there. Someday I'll tell you all about it."

"Never mind," said Rudy, as they stepped off the bus. "Just remember to be diplomatic with Dad."

"Oh, sure," said Eddie, "I know all about being diplomatic."

When the boys reached their home, they found their father sitting on the front porch reading the morning paper. When Mr. Wilson saw them, he put down the paper and said, "Hello, boys! Did you have a good morning at the pet shop?"

"We sure did," said Eddie. "Dad, can you make believe that you are the president of the United States?"

"Well, it will be hard," said Mr. Wilson, "but I can try. What's the game, Eddie?"

"Well, I'm the president of Tiddyhut," said Eddie, "and I've come to ask you if you would buy us a horse. You see, we have a lot of ice and snow in Tiddyhut, and we need a horse to pull our country's sleigh. We've just seen a very fine horse, a filly down at the pet shop. Her name is Dreamy, and she's beautiful. How about it, Mr. President? She's a bargain. Just two hundred dollars. A real bargain. Would you do that for my country of Tiddyhut? We'd be ever so grateful, and we could give you some very, very fine penguins."

Mr. Wilson looked at Eddie over his glasses. "Eddie," he said, "I gather that you have seen a horse and you want me to buy it to pull that old sleigh we have out in the barn."

"Well, something like that," said Eddie, and he stopped being the president of Tiddyhut and became Eddie Wilson. "Oh, Dad," he cried, "you never saw such a beautiful horse! She's a dream, and we've named her Dreamy. Do come and look at her, Dad."

"Not right now," said his father. "It's time for lunch."

At that moment, Mrs. Wilson opened the front door and said, "Come on, lunch is ready."

Mr. Wilson and the two boys went into the house. Joe and Frank were already in the dining room. "Wait until you see Dreamy," Eddie cried out.

"Who's Dreamy?" Joe asked.

"A beautiful little horse at Mr. Cornball's," said Rudy.

"I want Dad to buy her," said Eddie.

"I suppose you want the horse to sleep in your bed," said his mother.

Everyone laughed. "No, Ma," said Eddie. "I'll sleep in the barn with Dreamy."

"What makes you think she's going to sleep in our barn?" Mr. Wilson asked. "You talk about this horse as if it were ours."

"Oh, Dad," said Eddie, "what's the use of having a sleigh if you don't have a horse?"

"I'll think about it," said his father.

"Well, think fast," said Eddie, "because someone else could buy her real quick." Eddie snapped his fingers. "Just like that," he said.

"She's beautiful," said Rudy.

"I'll go have a look at her," said Mr. Wilson.

After lunch, the whole Wilson family piled into the car, and Mr. Wilson drove them to the pet shop. Eddie led the way to the stable, where they found Mr. Cornball feeding oats to Dreamy.

"Here she is, Dad," said Eddie. "Isn't she a dream?"

Mr. Wilson agreed that she was beautiful. But he said that he would have to think a long time about buying a horse that he hadn't even heard of when he had woken up in the morning. "I went to bed last night," he said, "not knowing that this creature existed. Now, before I go to bed tonight, I'm supposed to own her."

Eddie and his brothers all began coaxing their father to buy Dreamy.

"Two hundred dollars is a lot of money," said Mr. Wilson.

"Not for a horse like Dreamy," said Eddie.

"I'll have to find out more about her," said Mr. Wilson. "One doesn't buy a horse the way one buys a ball of string."

Mr. Cornball gave Mr. Wilson the name and telephone number of the filly's owner. "Mrs. Grayson will tell you all about her," he said.

Then the Wilsons climbed back into the car and drove home.

Later in the day Mr. Wilson called Mrs. Grayson, and they had a long talk about the horse. When he hung up the telephone, Eddie said, "You're going to buy Dreamy, aren't you, Dad?"

"I'm thinking about it," said his father. "Don't rush me."

"I'm not rushing you, Dad," said Eddie, "but don't you think you should call Mr. Cornball? Somebody else might buy her. You'd better call Mr. Cornball."

"Very well," said his father. "I guess we're going to have a horse."

"Hurrah!" cried Eddie and his brothers together.

Mr. Wilson dialed Mr. Cornball's number and the line was busy.

"Oh, dear," said Eddie. "It's probably someone else trying to buy Dreamy. I just know it's someone else who wants her."

Mr. Wilson kept dialing the number, and he finally reached Mr. Cornball. Eddie listened, and his heart sank when he heard his father say, "Oh, someone else is interested in buying the filly? How interested?" Eddie waited fearfully until his father said, "They'll let you know tomorrow? Well, I'm letting you know right now that I'm buying that filly. Mr. Cornball, you'll get my check for two hundred dollars first thing Monday morning."

Eddie jumped for joy. He ran around the room crying out, "Dreamy's ours! She's ours!"

When Mr. Wilson hung up the telephone, Eddie threw his arms around his father's neck. "Oh, Dad, it's wonderful!"

"Everything sounds good about that horse," said his father, "and she's already broken to the saddle."

"What's that mean?" Eddie asked.

Rudy spoke up. "It means she can be saddled up and ridden," he said. "I thought Uncle Ed would have to come up from Texas and break her to the saddle, but Dreamy's all ready to ride."

"Oh, boy!" said Eddie. "I can hardly wait."

Then he turned to his father and said, "Can we bring Dreamy home on Monday after school?"

"Not so soon," said his father. "We have to build a stall for her in the barn first. I'll get to work on it tomorrow."

Mr. Wilson needed a longer time to build the stall than he thought. Several weeks went by, but Eddie went to see Dreamy every day at Mr. Cornball's.

Finally, at dinner one evening, Mr. Wilson said, "I'm going to finish that stall tonight."

"Hurrah!" shouted Eddie. "Can I ride Dreamy home tomorrow?"

His brothers laughed. "Ride her home?" cried Joe. "You've never been on a horse in your life. Do you think riding a horse is like riding a bike?"

Then Eddie's father told them, "Mr. Cornball said that Mrs. Grayson would be happy to pick Dreamy up and bring her over in a horse trailer."

"Oh, great!" said Eddie. "I'll be right here when she arrives. I think Dreamy will like her stall. That's a good job you did, Dad. I won't forget to send you the penguins from Tiddy-hut!"

"Don't bother," said his father. "We have enough livestock."

"By the way, Ma," said Eddie, "don't you think it would be nice to have a bird? Mr. Cornball has some very nice birds."

"I'll think about it," said his mother. "It might be nice to have something that sings."

"Or talks," said Eddie. "Some birds talk."

"Four boys do enough talking," said Eddie's father. "You've talked me into buying a horse, and now, Eddie, you're talking your mother into buying a bird. What next?"

"A chameleon," said Eddie. "Uncle Ed's bringing me one the next time he and Aunt Minnie come for a visit."

Chapter 10

THE FIRE

THAT VERY NIGHT Eddie was awakened by the sound of the fire siren. He sat up in bed as he heard his father shout to his mother, "Fire someplace, Kate! I'm off."

Eddie jumped out of bed. His dogs Hippie

and Fritz fell off the bed and barked. Eddie was excited, for he knew his father was off to fight the fire with the other volunteer firemen. Eddie heard the car start and the tires squeal as the car rushed out of the driveway.

Eddie went to the window and looked out. His room was on the third floor, high enough so that he had a clear view of most of the town. Over it he could see a red glow. He watched and soon he saw a flame leap upward. Eddie became terribly frightened, for the fire seemed to be in the vicinity of Mr. Cornball's pet shop. "Dreamy, Dreamy!" Eddie cried aloud. "Oh, the puppies and the kittens. Oh, Dreamy!"

Eddie couldn't stay by the window. He rushed down to the second floor, where he found his brothers as excited as he was. "I think the fire is near the pet shop," Eddie cried. "I could see it from my window. I have to go. I have to see where it is."

The four boys rushed to their mother's room. They found her wide awake and looking frightened.

"Oh, Ma!" said Eddie. "I'm afraid it's the pet shop."

"Now, Eddie," said his mother, "don't imagine things."

"But it's over that way," said Eddie. "Ma, I have to go. I have to see. Just think of Dreamy and all those dear little animals." Eddie was crying, and the tears were rolling down his cheeks.

Now they could hear the sirens of fire engines. Eddie threw his arms around his mother and said, "Please, Ma, can you run us over in your car, just to make sure the pet shop isn't on fire?"

"Yes, I'll take you," she said. "You boys get into your clothes while I get into mine."

"Ma, you're wonderful," Eddie called back, as the boys hurried up to their rooms.

Eddie tried not to look out his window, but he couldn't keep his eyes away from it. The sky was red and there was a lot of smoke, but there were no flames leaping up into the sky.

Eddie put his clothes on very quickly and soon rejoined his brothers below. The four boys rushed down to the front door, where they found their mother ready to go out. In a few minutes they were all in the car, leaving two barking dogs in the house and one in the driveway.

The car soon neared the pet shop, and Mrs. Wilson and the boys saw that flames and smoke were billowing out and filling the road. But Eddie could see that the flames were not coming from the pet shop, and he cried out, "Oh, it isn't the pet shop! I think it's the carpet shop next door that's on fire."

Mrs. Wilson drove on until she was stopped by a policeman. "Can't let you through," he said. "We have a big fire here. All the nearby stores are being evacuated."

"What about the pet shop?" both Rudy and Eddie asked.

"Everything is out," the policeman answered.

"Where are the animals?" Eddie asked.

"I saw Pop Cornball carry some across the road. I think he lives there," said the policeman.

"Have you seen our horse? Do you know where Dreamy is?" Eddie asked.

"Just as I drove up," said the policeman, "I saw a woman ride off on a horse."

"Oh," cried Eddie, "who was she and how did she know about the fire and how did she know there was a horse?" Eddie was screaming.

"Quiet, kid! Quiet!" said the policeman. "Everybody in this town knows there's a fire. Just look at the people coming from all directions. The sirens woke up the whole town, and you ask me how the woman knew about the fire?"

"But the horse! The horse!" Eddie cried. "How did she know there was a horse?"

"Maybe it was her horse," said the policeman.

"It was our horse," yelled Eddie. "It's our Dreamy!"

"Well, sonny, you just be glad she took her away from here. Horses are very skittish at fires. You never know what they'll do."

"But she stole Dreamy! I just know she stole her. People steal things at fires. I've seen it on TV. She's a looter. That's what she is."

Eddie's mother put her hand on his shoulder and said, "Be quiet, Eddie. I don't believe she's been stolen."

"I don't think so either," said Rudy. "I think the woman was Mrs. Grayson. She probably came to take Dreamy to a safe place."

Eddie looked at his mother and said, "Do you think so too, Ma?"

"Yes, I do," she replied. "I think you'll find that Dreamy is safe."

Eddie felt comforted. "Well, let's see where the other animals are."

Eddie took his brothers across the street to the Cornball apartment. "Come on," said Eddie. "Let's go upstairs and see how things are."

The boys climbed the stairs, and at the top Eddie knocked on the door. They heard Mrs. Cornball call out, "Come in."

The boys went in, and Eddie cried out, "Oh, Mrs. Cornball, what about our horse Dreamy? A policeman said a woman rode off on her."

"Yes," Mrs. Cornball replied. "Mrs. Grayson came right away and took the horse back to her own stables where she'd be safe."

"Isn't that what Ma and I told you?" said Rudy.

Eddie waved his arms toward his brothers and said, "Mrs. Cornball, these are my brothers, Rudy, Joe, and Frank."

"Nice of you to come," said Mrs. Cornball.

"We were worried," said Eddie. "What about the other animals?" Eddie could see that Mrs. Cornball had two puppies in her lap, and three were rolling on the floor at her feet.

"All safe," Mrs. Cornball replied. "But smoke got into the shop, and the kittens and the rabbits seem very droopy. I'm afraid the smoke got to them."

"Do you think the puppies are all right?" Eddie asked.

"They seem quite spry," Mrs. Cornball replied, patting the two puppies that were in her lap.

Eddie went to look at two kittens that appeared to be asleep on the end of the sofa. "I hope they're all right," said Eddie. "I can see 'em breathing."

Eddie looked at two more kittens, sleeping on a cushion. "Poor little things," he said, "all choked up with smoke. I hope they'll come around."

"Where are the rabbits?" Rudy asked.

"They're in the kitchen," said Mrs. Cornball. "You can see for yourself how they are."

The four boys went to the kitchen. When they came back, Rudy and Joe were each carrying a rabbit.

"The rabbits choke every few minutes," said Joe, "but the gerbils and the guinea pigs are asleep."

"Where are the birds?" Eddie asked.

"They're downstairs in the real-estate office," said Mrs. Cornball. "The agent, Mr. Henry, was very kind. He opened up his office and told Pop to put any animals he had a mind to in there. Pop is very fortunate. He hasn't lost anything."

Just then Mr. Cornball came into the room.

"Oh, Mr. Cornball," Eddie cried, "I'm glad you didn't lose any of the pets."

"Not so far," said Mr. Cornball, "but I'm worried about the kittens and those two rabbits.

They need nursing. I won't have time to do much for them, because it will take Mrs. Cornball and me several days to clean up the shop. This fire has left a mess."

"Don't worry, Mr. Cornball," said Eddie. "I'll be glad to take the kittens and the rabbits over to our house, and I'll nurse them. They'll be OK, I promise you. My mother's downstairs in the car. I'll go ask her if it's all right."

Eddie clattered down the stairs. When he came back he said, "It's OK, Mr. Cornball. Don't worry. I'll take good care of them."

"Just keep them warm," said Mr. Cornball, "and keep the kittens on milk for a day or two. It's good of you to take them, because I'll have my hands full getting things shipshape in the shop."

When Eddie and his brothers got back home with the kittens and rabbits, it was two o'clock in the morning. Eddie put the kittens into a carton. He tried to get them to take some milk, but they turned away from it. "They must feel terrible if they won't drink any milk," said Eddie.

Eddie remembered that Mr. Cornball said to keep them warm, so he found some pieces of woolen cloth and placed them over the kittens, tucking them in carefully. Then he carried the carton upstairs and put it on the landing outside his bedroom door. Back downstairs he went to get a saucer of milk, hoping that the kittens would take some during the night.

On the way down he met Rudy, who had the rabbits in a box. "I put some lettuce in the box for the rabbits," said Rudy. "I hope they'll be better in the morning."

Eddie went to bed after he placed the saucer of milk in the box with the kittens. But he spent the rest of the night checking to see if the kittens were covered up. Every time Eddie got out of bed, the dogs fell to the floor. They didn't seem to like being disturbed.

The following morning the milk in the kitten box was gone, which Eddie felt was a good sign. He carried the box down to the kitchen and said to his mother, "Ma, I'll leave the kittens with you while I'm in school. I know you'll look after them."

"Rudy has just left the rabbits with me," said his mother. "Am I to look after rabbits and kittens all day? Now we have a Wilsons' pet shop."

"They won't be any trouble," said Eddie. "The kittens seem better. They're a little friskier this morning."

"Frisky!" exclaimed his mother. "Well, I'll look after them today, but I hope they frisk out of here tomorrow."

"Sure, Ma," said Eddie. "Thanks a lot."

"Now," said Mrs. Wilson, "I'm a cat and rabbit sitter," as she kissed Eddie good-bye.

By nighttime the kittens were livelier and were eating their food. Rudy reported that the rabbits were no longer choking. Both boys felt that their patients had recovered, but they had become so fond of the pets they wanted to keep them. Eddie and Rudy had already named the kittens A, B, C, and D, and the rabbits were named Jack and Jill.

On Sunday afternoon, Mrs. Grayson brought Dreamy to her new home with the Wilsons. The whole family was waiting outside to welcome Dreamy, including Eddie's three dogs. Rudy was holding the two rabbits, and Joe and Frank each had two kittens.

When Dreamy arrived, Eddie threw his arms around the filly's neck and said, "Welcome, Dreamy, to the Wilsons' home!"

His father patted the horse and said, "Welcome to the menagerie!"

"Oh, Dad," said Eddie, "I forgot to tell you. Mr. Cornball said we could have the kittens and the rabbits real cheap if we want them."

"And I suppose you want them," said Mr. Wilson.

"Oh, sure," said Eddie. "The kittens will be company for Dreamy. They'll be barn cats. They're cheap, Dad. It's a fire sale."

Then Eddie turned to his mother and said, "The canaries are reduced too, Ma."

Rudy laughed. "I guess you could call them firebirds," he said.

"That's right," said Eddie. "How about a firebird, Ma? You said you would think about a bird."

"Oh, I can see," said Mr. Wilson, "we're going to have a bird. Dogs, cats, rabbits, a horse, a chameleon, and now a bird! The place has been turned into a menagerie."

"That's right," said Rudy. "Eddie's menagerie!"

About the Author

Carolyn Haywood was born in Philadelphia and now lives in Chestnut Hill, a suburb of that city. A graduate of the Philadelphia Normal School, she also studied at the Pennsylvania Academy of Fine Arts, where she won the Cresson European Scholarship. Her first story, *"B" Is for Betsy,* was published in 1939. Since then she has written books almost every year and has become one of the most widely read American writers for younger children.